Other Books in
The Adventurers Series

For Michael, who loved Cornwall

Table of Contents

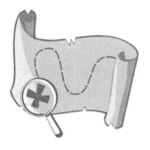

Chapter 1
School's Out for Summer

It is a curious truth that the last day of the summer term is a waste of time and energy for everyone involved.

Rules are relaxed on the last day of term, it no longer matters that a blue marker pen has exploded all over your white school shirt and your homework on Charles Dickens and Victorian London reads more like a review of last night's episode of *Eastenders*. The only rule followed is that nobody learns, or is taught, anything at all.

Lara Jacobs lifted her eyes at the clock and groaned. It seemed like her first year at Swindlebrook Secondary School would never end. Her classmates were sprawled out in front of a documentary about a paper factory. Some restlessly drummed their hands and feet whilst for others, the boredom had proved too much, and they laid face down over their desks almost comatose.

After what felt like an eternity, half past three arrived.

"What are you doing this summer Lara?" asked Daisy Duncely as she tried to catch up with her friend.

"I don't know yet... Mum's not really told us anything, but she said she's got a surprise to tell us tonight," replied Lara.

"My mum said your cousin is staying over," said Daisy.

Lara slowed her pace and sighed.

"Yeah," she said, "he lives with our grandma and grandad. They're going on a cruise holiday, so we're lumbered with him."

"Why isn't he going with them?" asked Daisy.

"You'd know why if you met him."

As Lara said goodbye to Daisy and walked up the path towards the front door, she felt a splattering of heavy raindrops on her head.

"Rufus," she yelled to her cousin, who was sitting in a tree, gleefully pouring water out of a rusty watering can.

"Your mum's being weird," remarked Rufus, who had jumped out of the tree with a thud and followed Lara into the house.

"Says the boy who sits in a tree pouring water on people. What are you talking about?"

"She's been making secret phone calls in her office *all* day long."

"They're not secret," said Lara, rolling her eyes. "She's working from home. To look after you, since you got kicked out of school."

"I *wasn't* kicked out," said Rufus. "I wanted to leave, and they let me go early."

"I heard you turned everything in the classroom upside-down, including all the chairs, desks, drawings, and your teacher's computer," said Lara, folding her arms. "And then stood on your head upside-down in the middle of it all."

"Well the teachers kept telling me I had to turn my life around!" protested Rufus. "So, I did."

It was true that Rufus' teachers had given him a lot of feedback.

Trying to teach Rufus some knowledge is like building a sand castle on the beach, wrote one teacher in his school report. *Some progress is made, but by the end of the day it's all been washed away and forgotten.*

Committed, focused and diligent, wrote another, *are three words that could never be used to describe Rufus.*

Later that evening Mrs Jacobs took Lara and Rufus to a pizza restaurant for dinner. Lara watched, appalled as her skinny cousin demolished everything on his plate in record speed. Mrs Jacobs' slice lay untouched on her plate. She cleared her throat and began the announcement that they had all been waiting for.

"Well, I have some news. I need to travel to Egypt this summer." Both Lara and Rufus dropped their pizza slices on their plates with a splat.

"Some very important artefacts have been discovered and need to be documented," said Mrs Jacobs. "Everyone else is out on summer projects so there's nobody else from the university that can go."

Lara's mouth opened and curled in disgust.

"What about us?" she asked.

"Oh, we'll be alright," Rufus chimed in, who was rather enjoying eating at fast food restaurants every night, combined with the general lack of parental supervision at Lara's house over the past few days. He had been quite relieved to offload Grandma and Grandad for five weeks, since Grandma had been scolding him constantly over the past few months. Having no adult relatives around all summer was an unexpected and delightful prospect. "We'll be able to look after ourselves, Auntie Sarah."

"I'm afraid that is quite out of the question," Mrs Jacobs said. "I'll need to be out of the country for several weeks, and you're too young to look after yourselves. How would you like to go to the Carl Kristie Kids' Camp?"

"They were fully booked months ago, Mum," said Lara, "Daisy couldn't get in this year either. Rufus is banned from going back anyway, remember?"

"Oh yes," said Mrs Jacobs, frowning as she recollected the call she received from Carl Kristie himself two summers ago to say that Rufus had stolen a rowing boat, pretending to commandeer a pirate ship. He had drifted far out into the lake, without any oars. All activities had to be stopped until two camp counsellors could drive out in a speedboat to bring him back to the shore. Even after Mrs Jacobs had driven him back to his grandparents' house, Rufus had talked in a pirate accent for several days.

"Ahoy me mateys!" cried Rufus, suddenly struck by the same memory. Lara put her head in her hands.

"Well, plan B it is then," said Mrs Jacobs. "You'll be going to your great-uncle Herb's."

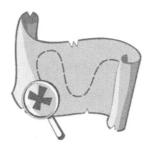

Chapter 2
Who is Great-Uncle Herb?

"*Who* is Great-Uncle Herb? And what about Barney?" asked Lara, wondering about her black, white and tan Border collie dog.

"Herb is Grandad's brother," explained Mrs Jacobs. "He has a great big old house on the coast in Cornwall. You'll love it. You can go swimming and fishing every day. Barney will go with you."

"You've never mentioned him before," continued Lara, leaning back in her chair with her arms folded. "I'm pretty sure he's never even sent me a birthday card."

"Me neither," said Rufus, his mouth full of pizza. "Eleven birthdays and Christmases… that's thirty-two presents he owes me." He stared dreamily at the thought of the bounty of gifts he was owed.

"Two elevens are twenty-two," Mrs Jacobs corrected. "And don't try your luck."

"I can't *believe* you're palming us off on a complete stranger," complained Lara.

"He's not a stranger, he's family," said her mother. "Really Lara, you're being very difficult about this. Rufus isn't making such a fuss."

"Well, he's used to being palmed off on other relatives."

The moment the words escaped her lips, Lara felt a sharp pang of regret in her stomach.

"*Lara,*" screamed Mrs Jacobs in embarrassment.

"Sorry Rufus," mumbled Lara, after a moment of silence.

"It's true," said Rufus quietly. "My mum doesn't want me, and Grandma says I'm tearing her nerves to shreds."

"Well…" Mrs Jacobs trailed off, struggling to deny the truth of his statement. "You'll always be welcome here Rufus, but this summer I just *have* to work. I'm sorry, really I am, but there's nothing else to be done."

Little else was said that evening, and Mrs Jacobs kept to herself the next morning. Lara and Rufus both sat in the living room, with Barney lounging by Lara's feet.

"Do you want to play games on my computer?" Lara offered, whilst still feeling guilty about the night before.

"I'm busy," said Rufus, jumping off his chair and walking towards the door.

"Busy? Doing what?" asked Lara.

"Your mum's shut all the doors downstairs and is going upstairs to the office, which means she's going to make a phone call she doesn't want us to hear," said Rufus.

"You're not supposed to listen to other people's conversations," lectured Lara, with a blush as she remembered the many times she had done this herself. "Do you *always* poke your nose into other people's business?"

"Only when it's interesting or if it affects me," said Rufus. "Or both," he added with a grin.

Lara's indignation was no match for her curiosity, and she quickly followed her cousin up the stairs, crouching beside him outside the small office.

"When did you even speak to him last?" the cousins heard Mrs Jacobs say on the phone. "Are you sure he's comfortable with the kids coming to stay?... Dad's taking them? But Dad hates that place and he thinks Herb's potty to still believe in all that treasure and curse nonsense..."

Lara was about to gasp until Rufus nudged her in the ribs.

"Tomorrow?"

"Come on, before she sees us," whispered Rufus to Lara, following her back towards the stairs.

That evening Mrs Jacobs instructed the cousins to pack their belongings as Grandad was coming to pick them up in the morning.

Lara wandered into Rufus' room where she found him body-slamming his over-stuffed suitcase.

"You forgot this," said Lara, picking up a book entitled *101 Greatest Schemes and Practical Jokes*. "I hope you're not planning to use this on me." She scrunched her nose up at the front cover illustrations of frogs, snakes and people screaming.

Mrs Jacobs came in and helped Rufus zip up his case.

"Mum, what's all this about treasure and a curse?" asked Lara.

"*Lara*. How many times have I told you not to snoop on other people's conversations?"

"I told her not to, Auntie Sarah," said Rufus, much to Lara's irritation.

"Well, it's silly really," said Mrs Jacobs. "There are all sorts of stories about a lost treasure somewhere around the house... all nonsense of course. It would have been found by now if it existed. Herb has spent a lot of money on it over the years, and absolutely nothing has ever been found. Grandma seems to think he's put it behind him now, thank goodness."

"And what about a curse?" asked Lara.

"There's no curse, such things don't exist."

"But you said –"

"Lara that's enough now, please," said Mrs Jacobs with a sigh. "I wouldn't be sending you to somewhere that was cursed, or doomed, or dangerous! Uncle Herb is a bit eccentric, but he's harmless. There's no treasure and no curse."

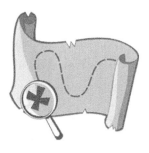

Chapter 3
Kexley House

The next morning it was soon time to cram into Grandad's car for the journey to Cornwall. Mrs Jacobs was relieved that Lara had lost her bad temper from the day before, although she still felt slightly nervous and had a few words with Grandad privately.

"Dad... I do hope everything will be alright at Uncle Herb's" she said. "You *will* let me know if things don't seem right over there?"

"Everything will be fine Sarah," assured Grandad. "You'll be able to speak to them on the phone, and I won't leave them there if there are any problems. Plus, Mrs Burt the housekeeper will be there every day; she has a child of her own who's the same age as Lara. They'll be looked after just fine."

Several hours passed in the car, with Grandad cheerfully singing show tunes. Lara decided this was even more grating than Rufus' various voices and accents, and buried herself in her book as much as she could. Rufus amused himself by furtively sending prank text messages to strangers from Grandad's phone, whilst Barney slept in his basket next to the luggage.

After several long hours, they drove into a small Cornish village and mounted a steep hill where the houses became fewer and fewer, and the sea sparkled over the cliff top. Finally, the car slowed down as they reached tall, old and very rusty gates. A sign on the left gatepost read *Kexley House*.

"That's your surname Grandad," said Lara in surprise.

"And mine," added Rufus.

"Yes, this is where I was brought up as a lad," said Grandad, "our family's lived here for generations."

Grandad stepped out of the car to push open the old gates then got back in to make his way through a winding narrow driveway. They passed a neat looking cottage just past the gate to the left-hand side. After the cottage, they turned the corner, and both Lara and Rufus' jaws dropped.

"It's not a house, it's a *castle*," said Rufus, bouncing up and down in his seat in excitement. "Herb must be a *millionaire*."

"Not at all," said Grandad, chuckling. "The old place needs a lot of work doing to it, Herb doesn't have the money, and neither do your grandma and me."

Grandad drove up to a large stone building with three rounded towers and a fourth tower almost in ruins, surrounded by a moat. Where the drawbridge would have stood was a tumbledown wooden bridge.

"Be careful if you go down the cliff path into the water," said Grandad. "The tide comes in quick, and the current can be very strong."

The car stopped outside the bridge, and a tall, smiling lady in a plain blue home-sewn summer dress ran out of a side door to greet them.

"Hello everyone, welcome to Kexley House," said the woman, in a strong Cornish accent.

"Hello Penny," said Grandad, giving the lady a warm hug. "Kids, this is Mrs Burt, she'll be looking after you while you're here."

"That's right," said Mrs Burt, beaming. "My Tom will be pleased to see you! He's twelve. It's wonderful to have you all here."

Just then a boy emerged from the side of the house pushing a wheelbarrow, wearing a dirty t-shirt and jeans—both covered in holes. As soon as he saw the group standing in front of the car, he swiftly walked towards them to help unload the luggage.

"Hi, I'm Tom," said the boy, smiling broadly, his brown eyes shining. The two introduced themselves while Grandad stepped aside to speak to Mrs Burt.

"Where's that brother of mine?" said Grandad, with a fearful glance at his watch.

"I saw him head out towards the moors this morning," said Mrs Burt. "He's been going there every day this week, coming back with seeds and what-not."

"Hmm," grunted Grandad. It had been a long time since he had spoken to his brother and he could not help feeling nervous leaving without speaking with him. "Well I best be off," he said, "I've got another few hours on the road, and Gran will have my guts for garters if I'm back late. We're boarding the cruise ship tomorrow."

"Why don't you come in for a quick cuppa?" offered Mrs Burt.

Lara thought Grandad was acting strangely. He kept glancing up at the house—but would not put a foot on the bridge.

"Thank you, Penny, but I must go. Rufus, Lara, you must promise me one thing—do not go into the south-west tower. The structure isn't sound, it's extremely dangerous, I–" Grandad's thoughts were interrupted by his mobile phone bleeping incessantly. He pulled it out of his pocket.

"Who is this?…Who are you?... Who are you calling a demented weasel…" read Grandad as he scrolled through his phone. "Well, how very odd…"

"They must have the wrong number," said Rufus, hastily opening the car door for Grandad. "See you after the cruise."

Grandad shrugged his shoulders as he said goodbye and drove back out of the gates, his phone still bleeping nonstop. Mrs Burt led the way back through the side door which opened up into a large kitchen.

"I expect you're eager to see your rooms," said Mrs Burt. "We don't get a lot of visitors here see, and most of the house is shut up. Tom, why don't you show Lara and Rufus their rooms, whilst I dish up tea for all of you? I'll give this pup here a bite to eat as well."

Leaving Barney behind with the welcome smell of food, Tom led Lara and Rufus through a narrow staircase and door into the main hallway. Beams of light streamed through the windows onto two statues of an Egyptian king and queen, more than three times the height of Tom, who was the tallest. Lara admired them, comparing both statues in her mind to the pictures her mother had shown her in university books.

"There's lots more weird stuff like that in this house," said Tom, noticing that Lara was lingering behind to look at the statues.

After turning to the left at the top of the staircase, they walked through a hallway that contained lots of pictures of people in old-fashioned clothes. All of the people in the portraits had jet black hair and dark eyes; bearing a striking resemblance to Lara and her mother. Shivers travelled up Lara's spine.

Tom introduced Rufus to a small bedroom overlooking the sea with just a few items of furniture and an antique globe on a chest of drawers.

They moved further down the corridor and to the right into what would be Lara's room. It was a lot bigger than Rufus', with a large four poster bed and a huge window overlooking the beach with a window seat. The wall opposite the bed was covered by a large tapestry showing Egyptian figures and symbols.

Lara marvelled at the size of the room and the view from the window.

"This *isn't fair*," Rufus complained, feeling hard done by.

"This room was Captain John Kexley's," said Tom. "He went to Egypt over a hundred years ago. That's where your mum is going, isn't it?"

"Yeah, it is," said Lara, wondering why her mother had never spoken about the connection between her work as an Egyptologist at the university and her family's ancestry.

"Hey Tom, do you know anything about a curse?" asked Rufus.

Tom shifted awkwardly.

"Who told you about a curse?" he asked.

"My mum was talking about it with my grandma," said Lara.

"Oh right," said Tom. "I'll see you for tea in the kitchen in a few minutes," he said, darting out of the door leaving Rufus' question unanswered.

Chapter 4
Strange Beginnings

"Mrs B, how can we get to the old tower at the back of the castle?" asked Rufus while munching a delicious warm Cornish pasty in the kitchen. He had longed to explore the old ruined tower the minute Grandad had warned them to stay away.

"Oh, that tower isn't safe dear, it's been locked up."

"Oh," said Rufus, disappointed though still believing he would find a way to explore the tower. "When's old Uncle Herb coming back then?" he asked, changing the topic in case Mrs Burt was going to ask him to promise not to visit the tower.

"He should be back around dusk," said Mrs Burt. "He likes his dinner late, so I leave something out for him in the oven. He's a… rather odd sort of person, your great-uncle; likes to keep to himself."

Just at that moment, the door swung open, and a very tall, burly man strode through the door and sat down with a heavy thud. His hair was black with specks of grey, and he had the same wide grin as his son.

"You're late," said Mrs Burt, scowling at her husband.

"What's for tea?" asked Mr Burt. "And who are these here kids? Did you finally bring back some friends from school Tom?"

"School finished last week, Dad," said Tom, blushing. "This is Lara Jacobs and Rufus Kexley."

"I told you that before," said Mrs Burt, whilst giving her husband a tap on the elbow with a rolled-up newspaper with every other word. "You've been down that Laughing Pig pub with Bill Stowes, and don't tell me you ain't."

"I ain't never lied to you my whole life, woman," argued Mr Burt. "What's the point of sticking around here? Three weeks I've been asking Herb to buy more packaging so we can start selling our crops, but no, he's too busy wandering around the hills collecting up wildflower seeds nobody wants! Fine way to run a business—would be nice to get some wages on time for once in this cursed place!"

"So you could spend it quicker down The Laughing Pig I suppose," said Mrs Burt, shaking her head. "You mustn't talk like that in front of the children. Tom, why don't you take Lara and Rufus down to the cove while there's a bit of light left?"

"Right," said Tom, bustling past the kitchen on the way to the door and scooping up Lara and Rufus by the arm on his way.

"My *pasty*," yelled Rufus after dropping his last piece on the floor, to see Barney hoover it up in an instant.

"Never mind that," said Lara. "Come on Barney— walkies," she called as she grabbed his lead.

"Sorry about that," said Tom as they crossed the bridge over the moat. "It's not good to be around when he comes back from The Laughing Pig, they always end up arguing about money." Almost as if to prove his point, they heard Mrs Burt behind them in the distance yelling at her husband. Her words became fainter as they headed across the lawn towards the path to the beach.

"Oh, it's alright," said Rufus, despite still mourning the last piece of his pasty. "All parents are nuts. As for my mum—well the less said about her, the better."

"Is your mum going on the cruise with your grandparents?" asked Tom.

"No," Rufus answered. "She's in Los Angeles."

"Wow," exclaimed Tom, for whom the idea of Los Angeles felt so remote it might as well have been Mars. "What's she doing there?"

"Acting," said Rufus without any enthusiasm. "Or that's what she says. I heard Gran on the phone saying she's mostly working in a diner and driving Uber taxis."

Lara remembered the last time she saw her auntie Rachel at a family Christmas party two years ago. Tottering from table to table in high heels, her aunt had boastfully told each group of people about the television projects she had worked on. She had not seemed to spend any time during the party with her son, who occupied his evening scampering around unseen, tying shoelaces together under tables and sprinkling table salt into every drinks container he could find.

"Well my mum's not nuts," she said, changing the subject quickly.

"Dad's not nuts either," said Tom. "You don't understand, he wants good things for my mum and me, but the vegetable business he's working on with your great-uncle... well, it's not quite working out. So, he goes to The Laughing Pig a lot."

"Why do you all stay here?" asked Lara.

"Mum couldn't bear to leave the place after all these years," said Tom, looking down at the floor. "And I like it here—I have to help with the grounds and stuff, but it's alright. Not many kids get their own private beach."

They headed across the lawn towards the steep path down towards the beach. Although the sun was setting, the air was still warm with a slight breeze. Tom was sure-footed and helped Lara and Rufus as they scrambled down the path.

Lara and Tom ran on the warm soft sand towards the shoreline being chased by Barney. Rufus hung back.

"I thought you said this beach was private?" he asked.

Tom and Lara turned around, noticing a figure with a cane had appeared on a rock towards the far end of the beach. As they edged nearer, they saw a man who looked to be in his eighties. He stared intently at the sea without acknowledging them.

"That's Uncle Herb?" whispered Rufus, looking at the old man's shabby waterproof coat and cap. "I knew he didn't have much money, but I didn't expect him to be a tramp."

"Watch your mouth," the old man snapped, still not turning his head towards Rufus. "And I'm not your uncle."

"How could he hear that?" whispered Rufus, even quieter.

"I've spent most of my life listening, boy," said the old man. Suddenly Rufus noticed from his eyes and the way he did not turn his head that he was blind. "The movement of the waves, the birds flying above; the wind as it blows; the dog's paws patting on the sand, the two others running towards the sea; it's not hard to see with just your ears, lad. Most people just forget to listen."

"Hello Sam," said Tom, moving forward and patting the old man on the shoulder. "How do you keep getting down here with your cane?"

"Pah," grunted Sam in response.

"This is Lara and Rufus," said Tom, after an awkward pause. "And their dog, Barney." As if to introduce himself, Barney jumped up the rock and licked the old man's face and hands. Sam's face creased to add even more lines to his face as he rubbed Barney's chest.

"Nice dog you have here," he said. "What are two children and a dog doing at Kexley House? Finally brought some friends home from school Tom?"

"No," said Tom, wincing at being asked this for a second time. "They're staying with Herb."

Sam stopped patting Barney and lifted his head in open-mouthed disbelief.

"Children inside the castle?" he asked. "Don't stay there, get yourselves out. It's no place for children, hasn't been for over a hundred years. Go back where you came from."

"What is it with people in this place?" asked Rufus sceptically. "Do they put something in the pints at The Laughing Pig? They're all stark-raving loony."

"Shut your mouth, boy," shouted the old man, who began to shake back and forth still perched on the rock. "The curse. The curse will get you like it did the others. Like it almost got me."

"It's just old stories," said Lara, "my grandad grew up there when he was a child."

"Aye and you won't catch him entering that castle again," said Sam, shaking his fists at the sky. "He'll *never* enter the place again. And neither will I. Not until they take back what belongs to them."

"Come on," said Tom, who seemed worried but not surprised by Sam's rants. "Back to the house."

Lara and Rufus lingered a moment, but the old man did not say anything further. Barney jumped down from the rock and followed them back towards the cliff path.

"Blimey, are we going to spend the next six weeks running back and forth between crazy people?" asked Rufus. "Come to think of it, your dad said something about this place being cursed too."

"That's right, he did," said Lara. "And you ran out when we asked you earlier. What's going on?"

"Don't worry about it," said Tom. "I wouldn't be here if the place was cursed, would I?"

"Well it's not like you have much choice," said Rufus, "and you don't have to sleep there."

"You're *scared*," said Lara, pleased at getting the upper hand over her cousin for once. "Worried the ghosts will get you?"

"Am *not*," cried Rufus. "You're the only one scared of ghosts. You screamed the place down last Halloween when I spooked you with my ghost costume."

"Cut it *out*," said Tom. "There's always been rumours of a curse… but nothing bad's happened. I don't really know where the stories came from."

"What about Sam saying that the curse almost got him?" Lara asked Tom, shivering slightly.

"I don't know about that… he does say some strange things though."

"And what about a hidden treasure?" asked Rufus. "Do you know anything about that?"

"Herb thought there was something, but I don't know anything about that either," said Tom. "He never found anything."

They were relieved to find only Mrs Burt left in the kitchen. After being given a glass of water each (and more warm pasties from the oven, much to Rufus' relief) the cousins made their way upstairs to their rooms. Both intended to stay awake for a while to think over the day's events, although they each drifted off to sleep within minutes. Only Barney stayed half awake at the foot of Lara's bed, keeping a watchful guard over his best friend.

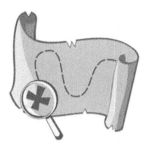

Chapter 5
Great-Uncle Herb

The sun streamed into Lara's room early, and she found herself feeling too energetic to stay in bed for long. From her window, she could see the waves glistening as they swept up to the shore. This time the beach was deserted, and there was no old man perched on a rock.

It was seven o'clock as Lara crept down the main staircase, expecting to be the only one up. She was surprised to hear voices from the kitchen and saw Rufus and Mr Burt in conversation. Mrs Burt was also at the table, piling bacon and eggs onto Rufus' plate.

Mr Burt looked almost a different person; his eyes were bright and frequently creasing with laughter. Rufus was busy making jokes whilst messily chomping on a bacon butty.

"Good morning Lara," said Mrs Burt, "sit yourself down and help yourself to breakfast." She pulled the chair out and patted the seat.

"What time did you all get up?" asked Lara.

"Well I'm up at half-past five every day," said Mrs Burt, "Rufus came downstairs as soon as I started cooking. Tom and Mr Burt have been up since dawn. Tom will be in for his breakfast soon."

Tom walked in at that moment, followed by a man in his seventies with thin, wispy white hair and round glasses. He did not seem to notice the two new visitors in his kitchen.

"Hello Herb," said Mr Burt, "are you coming to the farmer's market today? I'm loading up the truck in a few minutes."

"Not today, got visitors coming from London."

Everyone stopped and looked at Uncle Herb.

"You mean the children, Herb?" said Mrs Burt, using the same slow pronunciation that she had used with Mr Burt the night before. "They're already here, see? Lara and Rufus."

"Ugh?" Uncle Herb grunted, looking across the table. "Oh, you're here already are you? Thought they were coming next week Penny... no? Well, I wasn't talking about them, there's two visitors coming from the British Museum."

"I wish you'd tell me in advance of these things, Herb," said Mrs Burt, flapping her tea towel on the table. "You wouldn't have told me about the children either if your brother hadn't called me directly to make sure I knew. Why are two people coming from the British Museum, haven't you sold all the Egyptian relics from this house already?"

"What about those two big statues in the hallway?" asked Rufus, who always perked up at the mention of money.

"Did someone say something?" said Herb, glancing up without noticing Rufus.

"Yes, I said what about those two big statues," said Rufus, louder.

"They're not original, child," said Uncle Herb, who seemed to have no desire to learn new names. "Reproductions from the 19th century. Captain John Kexley probably had them constructed when he returned from his expedition. Anyway, the two visitors are staying at The Laughing Pig and heading back tomorrow. Something about Captain John Kexley and some research they're doing. They should be here just after lunch."

"Well, why don't you take your new friends to the beach, Tom," said Mrs Burt. "I'll pack you a picnic lunch for later. Best to stay out of the way, since Herb has visitors."

"Yes... stay out of my way today," said Uncle Herb, frowning as he realised he was buttering a piece of toast with the wrong end of his knife. "I'm very busy, and it's rather an inconvenience having children here… never liked nasty, noisy offspring, glad I never had any."

The cousins glared at their great-uncle, with Rufus resolving to think of at least a couple of good practical jokes to play on him.

Chapter 6
The Curse

After breakfast Lara, Rufus and Tom had fetched their swimming costumes and towels and headed towards the beach with Barney excitedly leading the way.

"What time does Uncle Herb normally have lunch, Tom?" asked Rufus.

"Well, he has his before me and my folks, so around noon, I guess. Why?"

"Just want to make sure we don't miss the people from the museum," said Rufus.

"They told us to stay *away* today," cried Lara.

"Exactly," said Rufus, with a smile. "Sometimes you really are a dope Lara, don't you ever want to know what's going on under your nose? Can't you stop being a goody two shoes for once? We'll start a watch at twelve-thirty. Tom, I'll take the first shift."

"Tom doesn't want to take part in your brainless schemes," said Lara. "And neither do I."

Rufus mimicked Lara's prim voice with a high-pitched squeal and Lara swiped him lightly with her beach mat. Barney, sensing a fun game, dived in between the two cousins jumping and barking excitedly.

"Don't you two ever stop arguing?" cried Tom, as he tried to get between Rufus, Lara and Barney. "I want to see what these visitors are all about as well; Herb isn't the smartest businessman, and we need some money for his and my dad's business. Herb will either take them to the study or his living room. Rufus—you stay low in the study and I'll hide somewhere in the living room. We'd better be there just after noon, so Herb doesn't see us."

"What about our lunch?" said Lara. "Your mum will expect us to go and eat lunch and you two will be hiding."

"Mrs B's doing a picnic lunch," said Rufus. "You pick it up and just say we're still on the beach." Lara rolled her eyes in reply, irritated that her role in the plan had been relegated to picking up food.

Lara's annoyance did not last for long as they spent a pleasant few hours on the beach, playing fetch with Barney and then swimming further into the sea. Grandad had been right about the strong waves, although all three were good swimmers and were careful not to let the current drag them further out than they wished.

Finally, Lara emerged from the sea to pour some more bottled water in a dish she had put out for Barney. She noticed the empty dish but did not see the dog anywhere. After calling his name twice, there was still no sign of him on the isolated cove.

"Rufus, Tom," she yelled, feeling a wave of panic rush over her. "I can't find Barney."

Tom and Rufus rushed out of the water; they both looked out to sea with a sense of dread, hoping that Barney had not run too far out in playing a game with his ball. Rufus turned and pointed behind Lara's back. She followed his gaze and saw Barney happily running towards her in front of Sam—the old man from the night before.

"Barney," she yelled, relieved. "Where were you with my dog?" she asked Sam. "He wasn't here on the beach, where did you take him?"

"I didn't take him anywhere, you daft girl," said Sam, heading slowly towards the rock where he had perched the night before. His right leg dragged heavily behind him as he walked across the sand slowly, with the help of a stick. "He's been on the beach the whole time."

"Come on, tell us where you were," whined Rufus. "And can you also tell us about that curse?"

"No."

"Why not?"

"I don't talk to foolish people."

"That doesn't make sense."

"Eh?"

"Well, you're talking to us now, so either you do talk to foolish people, or we're not foolish."

"You're foolish alright," said Sam.

"But you're still talking to us."

"No, I'm *not*."

"You *are*."

"Bog off you impudent cretin," snapped Sam, turning his back on everyone.

"Can't you just tell Barney what the curse is? You don't have to talk to us, we'll just listen," said Lara, trying to mediate between the annoyed man and her cousin. Sam did not respond.

"Well I can tell you about the curse, even if Sam won't," said Tom, winking at Rufus and Lara.

"Pah," Sam grunted, still with his back turned.

"Sam doesn't know much about it really, so it's better you hear it from me," Tom stated matter-of-factly. He noticed Sam clenching his fists. "When Captain John Kexley returned from Egypt, he accidentally ate a pork pie that had gone off. He caught a disease where you can't stop farting for days. The gas was so lethal people fainted all around him. Some even dropped dead. It was known as the curse of the pork pie. Nobody in the castle has been able to eat them since."

Lara and Rufus stifled their giggles.

"Well I heard something quite different," said Lara. "When Captain John Kexley returned from Egypt he tripped and fell off the boat when it docked..."

"Enough of this nonsense," scorned Sam. "Fine, I will tell you the curse, but don't come running to me when you ain't able to sleep at night in that cursed place. When Captain John Kexley was in Egypt, he rediscovered an ancient tomb. Inside that tomb were wondrous artefacts and treasures. A bitter fight broke out between Egyptian government officials and the captain over who the treasures belonged to. One night the authorities broke into the tomb after the workers had left, taking everything out of it. Many of the items were damaged in being so roughly pulled out of the ground after thousands of years. The captain was devastated, although there was a room with a blocked entrance that the authorities had missed, which still held precious lost treasures. He took them back to his house in Egypt and returned to England a few months later."

"Where's the treasure now?" asked Rufus, his eyes wide with interest.

"Nobody knows. All we know is that bad luck hit the Kexley family from that time on. An outbreak of scarlet fever spread on the Captain's ship during the passage home, killing his wife and two-year-old daughter. When he came back, all he had left was his twelve-year-old son who had been at a boarding school during his Egyptian excursion. Captain John Kexley never spoke of the treasure or where it was, but the curse was felt even after his death. His son, Robert Kexley, got married to a beautiful lady from Wiltshire. She died a year after their marriage, shortly after childbirth. Their child, Charles Kexley, died in his forties in a mining accident in one of the Cornish mines the family owned. Some kind of tragedy has hit every Kexley generation that's lived there."

"Wh–what about Herb's g-generation?" stuttered Rufus. "What tragedy happened?"

"I don't want to talk about it no more," answered Sam, dipping his head to the side and wiping a tear from his eye.

The three could not say anything for a few moments. They were frozen to the spot and stared at each other with open mouths. Nobody had the heart to question Sam any further. They each felt that there really was some truth to the curse that old Sam had warned them about. Lara shivered and felt cold, despite the warm sunshine of the July day. The thought of a family curse was not a pleasant one, and she suddenly longed to get away from the castle. She did not feel like talking about it to Rufus or Tom.

They stayed on the beach for a while longer, drying off on the warm sand. Nobody dared to mention the curse again, and Sam ignored them, getting out a harmonica from his pocket and playing slow, mournful tunes.

Finally, Tom noticed the sun high in the sky and realised that it must be almost lunchtime. He called Lara and Rufus, and the three headed back towards the lawn with Barney.

With the tale of the curse fresh in their minds, the towers of the castle rising above the sea no longer looked charming, but took on a more gothic and ominous appearance.

"Why would your mum send us to a place where people die?" Rufus asked Lara, with a shiver.

"They didn't die here, remember?" said Lara, trying to convince herself as well as Rufus. "Captain John's family died on the ship, and Charles died in the mines. It's probably still a coincidence anyway, loads of people died in the old days. And mum wouldn't have known anything about it. Grandad never told us about the place all these years until we came here. I don't know why Sam was so upset about it though… it's not like he knew any of those people."

"Let's find places to hide inside before those visitors come," said Tom, changing the topic as he sensed the cousins' unease. "It's just gone half-past eleven. Lara, we'll meet you here later."

With that, the two boys headed back to the castle and Lara sat down under a tree with Barney, trying to forget all about the curse.

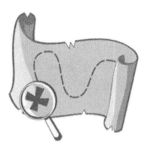

Chapter 7
The Visitors

Mrs Burt was surprised to see Lara by herself in the kitchen to pick up lunch, and hoped that she had not fallen out with Rufus or Tom.

"Your mother called this morning," she told Lara. "She didn't have long to speak, otherwise I would have gone down to the beach to find you. She's in Egypt and busy with work by the sounds of it; I told her you were both settling in well here."

Lara was disappointed to have missed speaking to her mother on the telephone, although she would not have spoken to her about the curse, she thought, as she would not have wanted to worry her.

Rufus had found a hiding spot in Uncle Herb's study in a built-in cupboard in the corner, whilst Tom was hiding behind a chair in the living room. Lara walked across the bridge to place the picnic basket behind a tree. She saw a taxi pull up and two men got out. The first to get out was a short, stocky man in his fifties, with balding grey hair. He was wearing a suit that looked a little too tight for him. He looked up at the castle and seemed to be assessing every window and patched repair. The second was a tall man in his early twenties with short black hair. He was dressed in a much smarter suit and was carrying two satchels and a box. Mrs Burt came out to politely greet the visitors. Lara watched as she shook their hands and they followed her into the kitchen.

Wondering what to do, she remembered that she had wanted to look again at the family paintings in the gallery and set off with Barney following behind.

A few minutes later, Lara surveyed each of the portraits until she found the one that she had felt most interested in seeing. The name underneath the portrait was printed in gold—*Captain John Kexley*. Her ancestor had a wry smile across his face and a knowing expression in his eyes that reminded her of Rufus, despite the captain's black hair. His brown eyes were similar to her own and her mother's. As she pondered the similarities, she heard footsteps coming from the other side of the gallery and grabbed Barney's collar to dive around the corner.

"Captain John Kexley's portrait is over here, gentlemen," said Uncle Herb. "A fine portrait painted a year after his return from Egypt."

Lara stood around the corner and peeped round to see the backs of her great-uncle and the two visitors. The shorter, older man was rubbing his hands together and had a greasy appearance. Lara was reminded of the used car salesman who had once sold her mother a faulty car.

"Very stimulating, Mr Kexley," said the shorter man. "So captivating to see the image of the man we have perused so much about. Perchance we might also catch a glimpse of the captain's diary? We understand that the artefact is in your possession, sir. It would be so delightful to examine his personal account of the voyages to and from Egypt. It would allow us to make the finishing touches to our journal article on nineteenth-century circumnavigation."

"Afraid not, Mr Bunce," said Uncle Herb flatly.

The younger man looked at Mr Bunce in dismay, who in return nudged him with a stern look. Uncle Herb stared straight ahead and did not seem to notice the exchange.

"And may I ask, Mr Kexley, why that might be? Is the document still in your possession?" asked Mr Bunce, his voice a little high and strained.

"It's currently on loan."

"Oh, interesting, it did not come up in our *research* as being on loan," said Mr Bunce, frowning again at the tall young man next to him. "Karim is new to our field of work. Pray, tell us, Mr Kexley, at which noble institution might we be able to view the artefact, perchance?"

Lara could not help feeling that Mr Bunce spoke and acted like a villain from a novel by Charles Dickens. He just could not get to the point without using five times more words than were necessary. She controlled the urge to laugh and stroked Barney's head as she held him back from running to meet the two visitors.

"At the village library," said Uncle Herb.

"That's easy enough then sir, we'll go and read it there," said Karim, speaking for the first time. Mr Bunce looked furious but could not give another hard nudge as Uncle Herb had turned around in surprise.

"It's not available to *read*," said Uncle Herb, bemused. "It's in a glass display case, and I have instructed the librarian not to let visitors handle it. Very old document, you know."

"Of course, of course," said Mr Bunce, resuming his grovelling demeanour. "Forgive Karim's ignorance, he is of course still learning, being but a student from Cairo University. I fear we have trespassed on your kindness long enough Mr Kexley; a thousand thanks for your hospitality. Kindly show us back to your study, and we will collect our belongings."

The three men walked back down the gallery, and Lara crept out and back down the stairs to wait outside for the two boys.

41

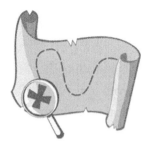

Chapter 8
Uncle Herb's Deception

Lara spread the picnic rug on the lawn close to the cliff overlooking the bay. A few minutes later, Rufus and Tom walked around the side of the castle and joined her.

"I never thought I'd say this—and it must be the first time it's ever happened—but you were right Lara," said Rufus, looking crestfallen. "They spent the first few minutes making small talk about the greenhouses before they left. Complete waste of time. I'm starving now," he said, eyeing the food.

"At least they were in your room for part of the time," said Tom. "I was hiding for ages for no reason, then when I came outside and saw the two walking to their car, all they talked about was going to the library."

"Well I didn't waste *my* time," said Lara, matter-of-factly.

"Why, what did you do?" asked Rufus. "Play cards with Sam? Learn to bake a pasty with Mrs Burt?"

"No," said Lara, still elated despite Rufus' sarcasm. "I overheard everything they said to each other in the gallery," she smiled, proud of her snooping skills.

Lara quickly repeated to Tom and Rufus the conversation she overheard between Mr Bunce, Uncle Herbert and Karim. The two boys listened with keen interest.

"Shame they're heading to the library now then," said Tom. "We'd never get there before them."

"I don't believe all that stuff about a research paper," said Rufus. "There's something fishy about them, especially that Bunce."

"Let's go to the library anyway," said Lara. "They can't take the book out of the library, and whatever it is they're looking for, maybe we can find it too."

The children finished their lunch and gave some leftovers to Barney, then packed up their picnic basket to take back to the kitchen. They quickly helped Mrs Burt wash up the lunch plates.

"What are you doing this afternoon?" asked Mrs Burt.

"Going to the library," said Tom.

"The library?" said Mrs Burt, pleased. "I don't think you've ever set foot in the library before Tom. Going to borrow some books, are you?"

"Er, yeah," said Tom, reddening. He was never good at lying.

"You won't find what you're looking for," said Uncle Herb, walking into the kitchen.

"But… I heard your visitors saying that they were going there?" said Lara.

"*Ha.* And so you thought you'd head there as well did you?" said Uncle Herb. "So much for Tom's sudden interest in reading."

"So why… what will… what if they…" said Lara, stumbling over how to ask about the diary without revealing that she had listened to her uncle's conversation.

"I know you were listening in the gallery, I could smell that dog of yours," scoffed Uncle Herb. "He really ought to take a bath. And no, they won't get their hands on Captain John Kexley's diary, even if they break into the library. The diary's not there."

"Where is it?" asked Rufus, almost bouncing with excitement. "Show us, *pleeeeaaase.*"

"Have a bunch of children playing with my ancestor's journal? Out of the question."

"If you didn't want to show it to anyone, why did you let those two guys from the museum come?" asked Rufus.

"I wanted to see if they were really searching for the lost treasure. Turns out they are. They won't be happy when they go to the library, and all they find is the castle's eighteenth-century cookbook."

"Nice," said Rufus, who appreciated any kind of trickery. "Show us the diary though, Uncle Herb. Maybe we can help you solve the mystery."

"I've been through the diary over and over, from cover to cover," said Uncle Herb. There's no mention of treasure, in fact, everything written in the journal is remarkably dull. Captain John was a clever man, he wouldn't have written anything in the diary that would directly lead to the treasure. It is probably written in code."

"Maybe we can work it out?" said Rufus, refusing to give up.

"Nobody can," said Uncle Herb with a sigh. "The secret died with Captain John. Many people in our family have wasted their lives trying to solve the mystery, and there is no point wasting any of yours." With that, Uncle Herb turned and stalked out of the kitchen, leaving Rufus feeling very frustrated and even more determined to get his hands on the diary.

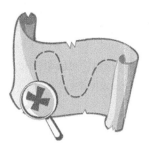

Chapter 9
The First Clue

That afternoon the sky turned a threatening grey. Lara had hoped to take Barney into the village, but as soon as she left the castle heavy raindrops fell from the sky, and she heard rumblings overhead. She turned and made her way up the staircases towards the top of the castle. As she looked out of a small window facing the sea, she saw great walls of waves sweeping angrily towards the cove and smashing against the rocks. There was no sign of old Sam.

She heard a steady thumping coming from Rufus' room and opened the door carefully, almost to be struck by a small, heavy rubber ball that Rufus was flinging around the room and catching.

"Watch where you're throwing that," Lara snapped, covering her head with her hands as she took a seat next to the two boys on the floor.

"What do you think those two goons will do when they realise the book in the library is a book of recipes and not the captain's diary?" asked Tom.

"I don't think they'll give up easily," said Lara. "Mr Bunce seemed quite determined. I don't think we've seen the last of them."

The three sat quietly for a few minutes, not knowing what to say or do next. They all felt dismayed that Uncle Herb would not share the diary and did not know where to start looking for it in the many rooms and chambers of the castle. Rufus, who was not able to sit still for long, once again launched the rubber ball against the wall. This time it bounced and veered left towards the window. Barney wanted to join in and jumped high to catch the ball in his mouth. On his way down his paws hit the globe standing on the chest of drawers and it rocked precariously, before falling to the floor with a crack.

The three were suddenly brought back to attention. Lara jumped up to check on Barney who had taken an awkward fall to the floor, but he sprang up excitedly, pleased with his triumph. He pranced around the room with the ball in his mouth and front paws springing, making muffled barks in joy.

"Barney you *idiot*," shouted Rufus.

"Don't blame him, it was *you* who threw the ball," Lara snapped.

Tom carefully picked up the globe, revealing a hole where it had crashed onto the wooden floorboards.

"It's fine," said Rufus. "We'll just turn it around and nobody will know. How many people need to look up, er, whatever country that was."

"No," said Tom, frowning. "My mum is fanatical about cleaning, she'll definitely notice. She doesn't miss anything."

"Maybe we can glue the pieces back on? Let me have a look."

Rufus carefully stepped over the broken pieces on the floor and held up one of them against the gaping hole in the globe. As he surveyed the damage, he noticed something behind the hole that appeared to be gleaming. He wrestled the ball out of Barney's mouth and held the excited dog back with one arm, whilst using his hand with the heavy ball to bash away at the hole. More pieces fell on the floor.

"Rufus, what are you doing," Tom shouted, "you're meant to be fixing the hole not making it bigger, I'm going to get in so much trou–"

"There's something inside," Rufus interrupted with enthusiasm. "Something shiny... I think I can get my hand in now."

Lara and Tom moved closer as Rufus wiggled his fingers inside the globe. He touched what felt like a piece of card, attached to a piece of string. The card would not move easily, so Rufus tugged it hard until it snapped away and he lost his balance, falling backwards.

Tom pulled Rufus up, and the three children examined the card in his hand. It was an old playing card with gold gilded edges, showing the Jack of Hearts. On one side of the card were two sets of numbers scratched across the card in thick black ink:

2.9.1862

10.20.23

"What does it mean?" asked Rufus.

"I don't know, but the Jack looks a bit like the portrait of Captain John in the gallery," said Lara. "He has the same expression too. It's like a cartoon version of the same person."

"The numbers could almost be dates, except the bottom one only has the decade and not the century," said Tom.

"But why would he write down two dates?" said Lara. "That doesn't tell us anything," she moaned.

Rufus snatched the card and jumped up, his face exploding with joy and excitement.

"The *diary*," he gasped. "It's the only thing that would have dates. Uncle Herb said there must be a code. Let's get it now."

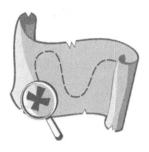

Chapter 10
Captain John's Diary

Lara, Tom, Rufus and Barney raced down the stairs, past the gallery and towards the great hallway with its imposing pharaoh and queen statues. This time they took the opposite staircase towards their great-uncle's study. The small number of visitors housed in the castle over the past thirty years had always been accommodated as far away from his study as possible.

As Rufus pushed open the door to the study, it slammed back with a loud bang. Uncle Herb turned in his chair and glared.

"What the blazes are you doing, charging into here like a pack of wild hyenas? Can't a man have any peace in his own home?"

"Uncle Herb," gasped Rufus, bent double with his hands on his knees, still wheezing from the sprint up and down stairs. "Give...us...the... diary."

"I most certainly will *not*," yelled Uncle Herb, his face turning red. "I will not have children charging into my study, making ridiculous demands for family heirlooms."

"Uncle Herb, you have to give us the diary," pleaded Lara. "We found a clue; it might lead us to the treasure."

"Oh, you found a clue, did you?" said Uncle Herb in mock wonder. "Tell me, *wise* children, where did you find such a clue?"

"I smashed the globe in my bedroom, and it was inside, see," Rufus fished the card out of his pocket and waved it in front of his uncle. Uncle Herb made a swipe to grab the card, but Rufus was too quick and dashed behind the sofa with it.

"You smashed the globe?" yelled Uncle Herb, his face now turning a disturbing shade of purple. "That is an antique, boy. I knew it was a mistake allowing you all to come, I will call your mother immediately and have you both sent home."

"Fine, we'll leave," said Rufus, feeling a surge of anger. "But if we leave, we're taking the clue with us, and you'll never find the treasure. Face it, Uncle Herb, you need us."

Tom and Lara moved to stand each side of Rufus— the three of them scowled at Uncle Herb across the sofa for a few tense moments.

"Arrrgh," cried Uncle Herb, flapping his arms in exasperation. "Share the clue with me, and I'll share the diary."

He held out his right hand to Rufus. Rufus turned to his left and right to look at Lara and Tom, as if he were a commander in chief and they were his military advisers. Each gave him a curt nod, and after a pause, he extended his hand to take the wrinkly hand of his great-uncle. They shook, and Uncle Herb turned to retrieve the diary from a shelf behind him, a thin smile appearing on his face that he did not allow them to see.

"Aw come on," whined Rufus, his hands raised to his head. "Are you serious, Uncle Herb? Your secret hiding place was on your *bookshelf* the whole time?"

"Well, didn't want to take my chances actually hiding it, did I?" said Uncle Herb defensively. "What if I forgot where I put it? Besides, people often don't search in obvious places when looking for things."

"Unbelievable," murmured Tom to Lara, shaking his head.

Uncle Herb put the book on the desk, and Rufus laid the card next to it. The book looked very old, its cover was a dark grey, and the pages were hard and crisp.

"I hope the card really is a clue!" said Lara, who did not think she could bear the disappointment of it being meaningless.

"It's something alright," said Uncle Herb. "Look!"

Uncle Herb opened the cover to reveal a picture on the first page that was identical to the Jack on the playing card. Tom, Rufus, and Lara gasped at the figure bearing a resemblance to Captain John, he had the same mischievous expression.

"Captain John Kexley was something of an artist, as well as a gamester," explained Great-Uncle Herb. "He often drew himself in this way, as the Jack of Hearts. Jack, you know, being a nickname for John. It's likely that he painted the portrait in the gallery himself. A man of many talents."

Lara was struck again with the thought of how her ancestor's expression reminded her of Rufus. She wondered if her cousin had the same thought as he peered at the drawing, his head tilted to one side.

"What do we have here? Two dates?" asked Uncle Herb.

"That's what we thought at first," said Tom, "but the second date doesn't match up with the format of the first."

"Hmm... the diary doesn't go as far back as 1823 in any case. Captain John was only born in 1832. Well let's try the first date in any case—the second of September, 1862."

Uncle Herb carefully leafed through the book and placed it down. Lara read the words aloud:

2ⁿᵈ September, 1862

Searched for a bookstall in Cairo, found a purveyor named Muhammad, whose stall was next to the spices shop. I then purchased some candles in the market. Played Faro in the evening with the archaeologists, laid my bet on Jack. Came from behind, won several hands then retired to rest. I will look for more spices at the market in the morning.

"It doesn't tell us anything," said Rufus, disappointed. "If anything, it's pretty boring."

"There's some kind of code here," said Uncle Herb, squinting.

The four of them stared at the numbers and the diary entry, hoping for some inspiration that would lead them to the hidden message.

"I'll be right back," said Rufus, darting out of the room.

"Strange," remarked Uncle Herb to Lara and Tom. "He seemed so interested in it, and now he runs off?"

Lara shrugged her shoulders. "He has a short attention span," she said. "His teachers are always complaining about it."

They continued to stare at the diary, and two minutes later the door burst open again with another sharp bang against the wall.

"Good grief, must you destroy everything in this castle, boy," said Uncle Herb, jumping up from his deep concentration in alarm.

Rufus pushed some papers to one side and slammed down a copy of *101 Greatest Schemes and Practical Jokes*.

"What is this nonsense?" scorned Uncle Herb.

"Rufus, mate, this isn't the time or place for jokes," said Tom, confused by his friend's behaviour.

Rufus flicked through the pages of the heavy book. Lara saw flashes of frogs and snakes on the pages and winced.

"This book has a part about code writing," Rufus explained. "It might help. See—*'Appendix - Secret Writing and Codes to Hide Your Schemes'*. Codes with letters... here it is—codes with numbers."

"Well I doubt my ancestors took hints from children's books, but we don't have anything else to go on I suppose," said Uncle Herb.

"Numbers, numbers... ok, I got it. Try this one—write a message with hidden words, count the order of the hidden words in the message and the corresponding numbers are the code."

"So, we need to find words ten, twenty and twenty-three," said Tom, running his fingers over the book.

*Searched for a bookstall in Cairo, found a purveyor **named** Muhammad, whose stall was next to the spices shop. **I** then purchased **some** candles in the market. Played Faro in the evening with the archaeologists, laid my bet on Jack. Came from behind, won several hands then retired to rest. I will look for more spices at the market in the morning.*

"Named, I, some? That doesn't make any sense," said Uncle Herb. "Got any more codes boy?"

"No, and the name's *Rufus*. The others are all to do with spaces and dots, so they wouldn't fit."

"So near and yet so far," sighed Uncle Herb.

Lara was dismayed, but still held onto hope. She picked up the card again, twirling it around in her hand. She turned it upside-down to see the same Jack figure the other way.

"Wait…" she said. "It's the other way around, Uncle Herb."

"So far and yet so near?"

"No… yes… I mean the code is the other way around," Lara spluttered. "Just as the playing card shows the Jack the other way around. Start from the back."

Tom quickly put his fingers on the diary again, mapping out the words backwards on the page.

Searched for a bookstall in Cairo, found a purveyor named Muhammad, whose stall was next to the spices shop. I then purchased some candles in the market. Played Faro in the evening with the archaeologists, laid my bet on **Jack**. *Came from* **behind**, *won several hands, then retired to rest. I will* **look** *for more spices at the market in the morning.*

"Jack, behind, look… look behind Jack," yelled Rufus. "That sounds like a clue."

"My goodness, I do believe you children did it," said Uncle Herb. "Look behind Jack… the portrait," he said while rubbing his chin. "Something must be behind the portrait. To the gallery, let's go."

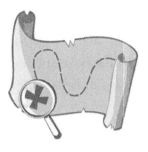

Chapter 11
The Painting

Two minutes later Tom, Lara, Rufus, Uncle Herb and a perplexed Barney were standing in front of the portrait of Captain John Kexley. Barney was not sure why they had been racing across the castle, but he always enjoyed anything that seemed like a game. Rufus raised his hands towards the painting, but his uncle put a hand out to stop him.

"Leave this to me, boy," he said, still wheezing. "I know your propensity towards destruction. This is best left to a safe pair of hands."

Uncle Herb carefully unhooked the portrait from the wall, and Tom helped him to lower it to the floor. Dust filled the air from behind the painting, causing both Barney and Rufus to snuffle and sneeze.

Tom wiped the back of the painting with his sleeve, making it even grubbier than it appeared before. He then moved the small markers to slide the wooden cover away from the back of the canvas. There was nothing marked or hidden.

"Well… the diary did say look *behind* Jack, maybe there's something on the wall?" suggested Lara. She patted her hands on the space behind the wall, but felt nothing. Rufus tapped the wall to try to sense if there was a space behind, without any luck.

"It seems we've become unstuck," said Uncle Herb with a sigh. "There really is nothing here. Do you suppose we had the wrong clue?"

"I don't know," said Tom, scratching his head. "Are there any other portraits of Captain John?"

"None that still exist here," said Uncle Herb. He picked up the painting and carefully put it back on its hook. "Well, that really was a bit of excitement children, but I'm afraid we've come to a dead end. It's not easy digging up the past of over a hundred years ago." With that, he walked slowly away, leaving them feeling sad and disappointed.

"I felt so sure we'd find something," said Lara. "Maybe the clue was already taken?"

The storm had since passed, and it was safe to venture outside. Tom and Rufus played with a football towards the back of the castle, whilst Lara decided to take Barney for a walk. She walked towards the beach path and saw Sam once again—this time he was walking slowly along the shoreline with his stick. Lara did not feel up to another encounter with the angry old man, so she turned to walk in the opposite direction towards the village.

The village was bustling as Lara turned the corner, with villagers either heading home to their houses or across the street to The Laughing Pig. She did a loop of the area, noting the pretty houses and gardens with their neat white fences and rows of flowers. She came up to a path leading to a small red brick building, which housed the village's library. A lady in her sixties wearing a matching yellow cardigan and skirt was locking up the main entrance and shuffled towards Lara.

"Hello," she said brightly, stopping to stroke the back of Barney's head. "Nice dog you have here. What's his name?"

"His name's Barney."

"Hello Barney," said the librarian, rubbing Barney's side with eagerness. "You don't sound as if you're from around here?"

"No, I'm not; I'm visiting my great-uncle with my cousin, we're staying with him at the castle this summer."

"Oh yes, dear me, Mrs Burt told me she was expecting you. We don't get many visitors in these parts, although you're the third I've met today."

"Oh yes?" asked Lara, immediately thinking of Mr Bunce and Karim.

"Yes, although the other two weren't as pleasant as you, dearie. Two very odd fellows came in the library asking for documents relating to Captain John Kexley. I showed them the book of recipes we have in the display cabinet from the castle's old days, as well as a book containing the history of the village. Then they behaved most astonishingly—one of the chaps slammed down the history book, cursing and muttering under his breath, and stormed out of the library without so much as a goodbye or thank you. They had been fairly pleasing up to that point. Some people have no manners. Well, I'm off home, nice to meet you and young Barney here."

The librarian rounded the corner and Lara headed in the opposite direction back towards the castle. She wanted to tell Tom and Rufus that as they expected, Mr Bunce and Karim were displeased at being tricked by their great-uncle.

Half an hour later, when Lara walked back in the kitchen, she saw her cousin and Tom seated at the table. Tom had a worried look on his face and looked up at Lara as if to shoot her a warning. Lara turned to see Mr Burt standing with his back towards her and quickly slid onto the bench to take a seat beside Tom before she was noticed.

"What did I tell you about your drinking at The Laughing Pig with Bill Stowes?" said Mrs Burt, shaking her fists at her husband. Intoxicated in front of the children again! Shame on you, Alfred Burt."

"I am not intoxicated, believe me," said Mr Burt. In his defence, he did not have the same red, ruddy appearance of the night before. "We didn't stay down there long. Got quizzed by two strangers I didn't like the look of, so we picked up and left."

"What strangers, Mr Burt?" asked Rufus.

"Some chubby man who talked funny and a foreigner," said Mr Burt, taking a big bite of the baguette in front of him.

Lara, Tom and Rufus exchanged looks and nudged each other under the table.

"Why, we had them here today," said Mrs Burt. "Didn't think much of them either. What were they asking you Alfie?"

"They were here? Funny, they didn't mention that. Asking something about a book and then if the owner of the house ever travels out of the village."

"What did you tell him, Dad?" asked Tom.

"Don't know why you're all so interested," said Mr Burt, looking up from his baguette and soup to notice that everyone was staring straight at him. "Told them I haven't ever read any of the books in the castle; don't have time to read books at all these days. Told them Herb hasn't left the area in years."

The children gave each other another worried glance. Mrs Burt put three bowls of soup in front of them, which they finished quickly, longing to talk to each other outside of the kitchen.

"So, they're still fishing around," said Tom, after they had helped Mrs Burt tidy up and turned the corner around the kitchen.

"I don't like it," said Lara. "I met the librarian in the village earlier, she said they were angry that the diary wasn't there. Still, I don't see why they'd stick around, especially since they've got no more to go on than we have."

"I'm heading home," said Tom. "I'll see you guys tomorrow. Let's have another look at the painting when there's daylight, you never know, maybe we missed something."

Lara and Rufus headed upstairs to sit in the living room near their bedrooms. Rufus had retrieved his practical jokes book from Uncle Herb's office and was studying it in detail.

"I wish you'd stop reading that," said Lara, squirming. "I don't want to wake up and find a frog in my bed or something."

"I'm not reading it for your benefit," said Rufus. "Thought I'd read up again on the codes section in case there's something useful. Like Tom said, we'll have another think about the clue tomorrow."

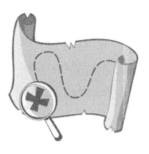

Chapter 12
A Surprise in the Morning

The children went to bed, Barney nuzzled against Lara's feet. Despite the questions floating in her head about the clues and the painting, for the second night in a row, Lara was tired from the excitement and soon drifted into a heavy sleep. Halfway through the night she woke up to Barney growling, but sleepily nudged him with her foot and fell back asleep. She woke up the next morning at seven o'clock. After she had washed and dressed, she went down to the kitchen followed by Barney. They were greeted by Mr and Mrs Burt, Tom, Rufus and Uncle Herb who were standing with two tall, burly policemen.

"What happened?" asked Lara, surprised and concerned by the look of worry on everyone's faces. "Is everyone alright?"

"We had a break-in last night," said Mr Burt, who was pacing up and down. "They broke in the greenhouse around the back and stole a painting in the gallery."

"Captain John Kexley's portrait, to be precise. Look here," said Uncle Herb, turning to the policemen. "As I've told you, we know who did this. They were here yesterday, and they've come back for the painting. You should be at The Laughing Pig now questioning them."

"Unfortunately, sir, they've already left," said one of the policemen, a tall young man in his twenties with a thick Cornish accent. I took the liberty of stepping out to call the landlord a few minutes ago, who said they paid their bill last night and checked out very early this morning before anyone saw them leave. And as we suspected, there are no fingerprints in either the greenhouse or the gallery. We've contacted the British Museum and will have some of the London officers investigate. Here's my contact details Mr Kexley; we'll keep looking, but if you think of anything else, please give me a call." The policeman handed Uncle Herb a card and turned to leave.

Uncle Herb watched the two policemen leave and slammed his fist on the kitchen table in annoyance. The children were equally frustrated. Only Mrs Burt seemed to look composed as she busily clattered around the kitchen cupboards until she pulled out a tea set.

"I'll get you all a nice cup of tea. Makes everything better, so it does," she said.

"Not this time I fear, Penny," said Uncle Herb solemnly.

"Oh, I don't know about that," said Mrs Burt, trying her best to be cheerful. "Things come and go you know, but it's people that matter the most. Not that I won't miss that painting, seeing that I've been dusting it all these years, you know. Collect a lot of dust, see, old paintings, so they do."

Uncle Herb sunk his head further into his hands. Nobody wanted to listen to Mrs Burt telling a story about dust, but she continued with enthusiasm.

"My old mam used to dust this place too you know, and her mam before that. Why, my mam used to dust that painting just as much as I did. My grannie, well she dusted it when the painting was still in its old place in the south-west tower, never believe the amount of dust on the old relics in this place. Dust collects all over—"

"What did you just say, Mum?" asked Tom, who had only been half-listening up until that point.

"Oh, I don't know Tom, I was just talking about dust."

"Yeah, not that—you said the painting used to be *somewhere else*?" Lara, Rufus and Uncle Herb perked up, whilst Mr Burt looked just as bored.

"Why yes, it used to hang in the south-west tower."

"Where, Mrs Burt? Where did it hang?" questioned Uncle Herb, standing up and clutching the table.

"Well I can't be sure of the exact spot, but my mam said it was taken down when the south-west tower was closed off. Now I bet that old tower has collected a lot of dust…"

Without a word, Tom, Rufus, Lara, and Barney raced out of the room with Uncle Herb following at a slower pace behind. Mrs Burt turned from the stove to look at her husband in bewilderment.

"Was it something I said?" she asked.

"Haven't the foggiest" replied Mr Burt. "Bonkers, the whole lot of 'em."

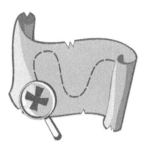

Chapter 13
The Tower

Lara, Rufus, Tom, Barney and Uncle Herb made their way to the south-west tower towards the back of the castle, which had been closed off due to its state of disrepair. The door to the staircase was locked, and Uncle Herb took out a chain of keys from his back pocket.

"Children, you must be *very* careful going up these steps," he warned, flicking through the keys slowly. "It's not safe, and the steps and walls could give way at any moment. There was an accident here many years ago, while I was away at school. Follow behind me."

The three grew impatient as Uncle Herb seemed to take an age to select the right key. He finally selected a long rusty key but had trouble turning it in the lock. Tom stepped in and turned the key, but the door was still stiff and would not open. He braced himself and barged it open with his shoulder. The whole tower shuddered with the impact.

"Right," said Uncle Herb, a little nervous. "No sudden movements... follow me. You'd best leave the dog here, push the door to stop him following us."

Uncle Herb led the way up a steep winding staircase, leaving Barney whimpering behind the door. Several steps had worn away, and with no handrail, they had to carefully keep their balance as they mounted the steps. Holes had formed in the walls, and the cold air, as well as the view of the drop below, made everyone shiver.

All of a sudden, Uncle Herb stopped so abruptly that Tom almost barged into him. They both looked down and saw that a large part of the wall was missing, including part of the step.

"What's the holdup, let's go," cried Rufus, who was behind Tom.

"There's a hole, be *very* careful," said Uncle Herb, as he gingerly stepped over to the next step and sighed in relief when it did not give way. Tom followed him, then turned back to give Rufus and Lara a hand. Lara was about to take Tom's hand when her back foot slipped. She let out a scream before Tom managed to pull her up to the next step.

"For pity's sake, be careful," cried Uncle Herb.

They continued up the steps and finally reached another door. This door was smaller and unlocked, and Uncle Herb pushed it open with less difficulty than before.

They stepped into a round stone room that was completely bare except for another staircase that led to the top of the castle. The steps had crumbled completely and looked too unsafe to attempt to climb.

They looked around the room and peered through narrow slits in the wall, where the cliff dropped straight into the sea.

"How do we know where the painting was, there's nothing here?" asked Lara.

"Let's all work our way around this room," said Uncle Herb. "Search for any kind of sign of anything that looks different."

The four each took a different part of the wall and carefully studied it for any clues of where the painting had been. Several minutes passed, and the children and Uncle Herb became impatient. Then Rufus felt his hand touch something a little different in the wall.

"Here," he shouted. "There's a hole in the wall, it looks like they could have hooked the painting here."

The others gathered around and looked at the hole where Rufus was pointing. He smoothed his hands across the wall. It felt rough and heavy. Suddenly he felt a crack that was barely visible. He followed the line of the crack around a small rectangle.

"There's something here," Rufus said. "I wonder if we can pull this rectangle out completely."

Uncle Herb slid an ornately decorated pocket knife out of his trouser pocket and handed it to Tom. "Try this," he said.

Tom started sawing the crack in the wall with the knife. It seemed that a lot of debris had filled it, which eventually started to fall away as the stone became loose. Tom then carefully used the knife to wedge the stone out of the wall. Once it stood out a few centimetres from the wall, he was able to lift it out whole. The stone was about the same size as a brick in Tom's hand.

To Tom's irritation, Rufus darted in front of him to put his hand in the hole. He pulled out a small, dark wooden box, fastened shut by a metal clasp. On the front of the box were the initials *JCK* in curly, thin gold letters.

"John Crispian Kexley," said Uncle Herb.

"A clue, it *has* to be the next clue," cried Rufus, his eyes beaming with excitement.

"Before you open this we need to go back downstairs," said Uncle Herb. "The wind is picking up in this tower, and I don't feel comfortable about us all being here. We also need to treat this box very carefully; the last thing we want is for the contents to be damaged. Tom, hold the box inside your jacket, and we'll go to my study."

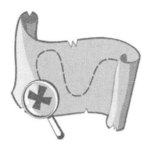

Chapter 14
The Box

Tom, Lara, Rufus and Uncle Herb went carefully back down the stairs where Barney was very relieved to see them, following them towards the study at the other side of the castle. They each took a seat on the old burgundy leather couches and armchairs. Tom took the box out of his jacket and once again looked at the initials *JCK* etched in curly decorative print. He looked up at Uncle Herb who nodded to tell him to go ahead. Tom slid his fingers around the tiny clasp, his heart beating fast and his hands trembling. Inside the box was a purple silk lining and a folded piece of paper. He unfolded the paper as the others crouched nearer to get a better view. Inside was something black and crumbly. It almost turned to ash.

Uncle Herb took the box from Tom and felt the black substance with his hands, then sniffed it. His face contorted in disgust.

"Tobacco," he said, almost spitting the word out. "We have discovered Captain John Crispian Kexley's secret tobacco hiding place. Tom, check to see if there's anything else in here." Uncle Herb handed the box back to Tom, who felt his way around the silk and inspected the outside of the box for other clues. There was nothing other than the initials JCK.

"Nothing else in here," he told the small group, who all felt very downcast.

"I fear that we are coming to another dead end," said Uncle Herb. "I'll look through my old family papers to see if I can find anything relating to the painting. You know, I wonder if there was a second clue actually within the portrait, but now those blasted thieves have taken it we'll never know."

"Would you like us to help you search your papers Uncle Herb?" offered Lara.

"No, my papers are in disarray, and it's best I do it alone. Leave me now." Uncle Herb turned to his desk, feeling sad at yet another disappointing outcome in the many years he had spent trying to discover the secrets of his ancestors.

For the rest of the morning, Tom went to complete his chores around the castle, watering the plants in the greenhouses and picking the ripe tomatoes and vegetables. Lara took Barney for a quick walk around the grounds, whilst Rufus wandered around the castle in a state of unrest. He was too annoyed about the box and dead end to focus on anything else.

At lunchtime, they met in the kitchen to eat a feast prepared by Mrs Burt. Rufus greedily eyed the thick bread and butter, baked potatoes, ham, cheese, scotch eggs and salads. The sight of food was always enough to lift him out of a bad mood. Tom poured lemonade into three glasses and found biscuits for Barney.

"Herb seemed pretty upset about the box and map," said Lara.

"The castle's been losing money for years," said Tom, "maybe he thought if we found the treasure the debts could be paid off and some repairs made to the building. Things aren't looking good."

"But we can't give up now," said Rufus. "There's still some leads... What about Mr Bunce and Karim? They haven't disappeared into thin air, and the clue was probably in the painting. Or behind it at least."

"Well they were last seen at The Laughing Pig," said Lara. "Why don't we head down there? Maybe the landlord will tell us something that the police missed."

"It's worth a shot," said Tom. "It gets us out of this place anyway, and maybe Herb will have found something by the time we get back."

The children finished their drinks and left the kitchen. They passed Mrs Burt outside the door where she was hanging washing on a line.

"Where are you off to?" she asked, as the children hurried past her quickly.

"To The Laughing Pig pub," said Lara.

"Oh, alright," Mrs Burt replied, absent-mindedly before realising what she had heard. "Wait a minute, you're going *where*?"

"She said we're going to the yacht club, mum," said Tom.

"Oh," said Mrs Burt to herself, as they hurried away. "Good gracious, I must have that flaming pub on the brain."

Chapter 15
The Laughing Pig

Lara, Rufus and Tom entered the pub through the old oak door with Barney following close behind. The Laughing Pig was a small, narrow public house with low ceilings and painted black beams. The red carpet looked as if it had seen better days and the sandy coloured wallpaper was mostly covered in paintings and old farm equipment.

"Hello Peggy," said Tom to the young barmaid at the bar. "Are Mr or Mrs Pengilly in?"

"Mrs Pengilly's upstairs," said Peggy. "I'll go and fetch her."

The blonde barmaid left through a door at the back of the bar.

"Tom, what are you kids doing here?" boomed a voice from behind them. Tom turned to see his father sitting at a table by the door with another equally rugged looking man.

"Hello Dad, hi Bill," said Tom, sheepishly. "We're just here to see Mrs Pengilly."

"You know your mother doesn't want you in here," said Mr Burt. "Wait till I tell—"

"I don't think she wants *you* in here either Mr B," Rufus interrupted. "If you didn't see *us*, then we didn't see *you*."

Bill Stowes chuckled into his glass of ale as Mr Burt frowned.

"Cheeky so-and-so," said Mr Burt, pondering for a few moments. "Fine," he said reluctantly, "we'll say no more about it then."

Just then, a woman in a trouser suit carrying an accounting book followed Peggy through the door to the bar.

"Hello Tom," she said, "what brings you here? Come to fetch your dad?"

"No, Mrs Pengilly, we wanted to talk to you about some visitors you had."

"Well let's not stand here much longer, you're too young to be at the bar. We'll go into the function room. Peggy, bring some of that saffron cake in would you, and something for the kids to drink. And a bowl of water for the dog."

The children all thanked Peggy and followed Mrs Pengilly into a room to the side of the bar. It was large and held a number of tables with a large stone fireplace. The walls were covered with more paintings, mostly naval pictures of ships and the coastline. Peggy came in and handed the children orange juice and thick slices of cake. She laid a bowl of water on the floor with a dog biscuit; Barney licked her hand gratefully.

Tom began to tell Mrs Pengilly about the theft of the painting and their suspicions of the two guests that had stayed at The Laughing Pig. Mrs Pengilly listened intently but did not seem surprised.

"The police asked me if they were still here first thing this morning," she said, "but they'd already gone. One of them left his room in a right state; bits of rubbish everywhere. I didn't like them much, the younger gentleman seemed nice enough, but the older chap was very smarmy." She turned up her nose. "Asked us all sorts of questions about everything you could think of. I didn't like to tell him much; he had a creepy way about him and talked ever so funny, as if he were from olden days and trying to sell me something second-hand."

"Did you see them come in late last night?" asked Tom.

"They were sitting in the bar drinking until closing. Rather annoying as they were turning off a lot of my regulars, interrogating them all with questions. If they did take the painting, they would have slipped out after closing."

"Did they say anything about where they were going?"

"Well… Karim mentioned something about a train journey, but the older chap shut him up straight away. I'm sorry, but I don't think there's much else to tell you I'm afraid. I do hope the police catch up with them."

They finished their cake as Mrs Pengilly changed the topic to life at the castle.

"Uncle Herb and Dad's business isn't going so well," said Tom, "Dad gets in a mood about it sometimes. Things will pick up though."

"I hope so," said Mrs Pengilly with a frown. She had often heard Alfred Burt cursing the poor state of affairs at the castle. "I must get back to my bookkeeping, stay and finish off your cake."

"What is this room used for?" asked Lara, as Mrs Pengilly got up to leave.

"Oh, the yacht club and other societies have meetings and functions here from time to time. It doesn't get much use since the olden days when people played cards in here."

"Cards?" asked Rufus.

"Yes… older games that aren't played anymore. Basset and Faro were the main ones."

"Did Captain Jack Kexley play card games in this room?"

"As a matter of fact, he did," said Mrs Pengilly. "This pub has been in my family for generations, and I've heard that he would win and lose a lot of money here. I must go, or I'll never get these books done; come and see me another day."

Mrs Pengilly left the room and Lara and Tom stared at Rufus.

"Why were you asking about Captain Jack Kexley?" asked Lara.

"She mentioned Faro… Captain Jack Kexley mentioned the same game in the diary."

"You're right… I wonder if there's some clues in this pub since he spent so much time here?"

"I think I can see one already," said Tom. "Look over there—that looks familiar too."

Tom pointed behind Lara and Rufus. For a moment they did not notice what he was pointing at as the walls were so cluttered with paintings and objects. Their eyes were first drawn to a large painting of a sea wreck over the fireplace, then pictures of landscapes, then a couple of old-looking cartoon pictures of characters from old newspapers.

Then they saw it. Behind a chair, almost out of sight, was a picture of the Jack of Hearts. It mirrored the card that the children had found in the globe and the picture in the diary.

"Look behind Jack… do you think that could be it?" asked Lara.

The three children jumped out of their seats, Tom looking cautiously behind him in case either Mrs Pengilly or Peggy returned.

Lara carefully lifted the picture from the wall and turned it over. The back of the frame was coming away from the picture already, with nothing behind it. They then turned their attention to the wall. Behind the pictures, the walls of the room were covered in small square wooden panels. The picture uncovered a panel that looked slightly more faded in colour than the rest. Lara placed her hand on the panel and gently pushed it forward. The panel did not move, so she increased the pressure of her hand slightly.

"Hurry up," said Rufus, who could barely keep himself from pushing his cousin out of the way to try it himself.

Lara frowned but continued pushing the panel. All of a sudden, she heard a click, and the panel moved back fast. At the same time, she heard a grating sound. Rufus and Tom went to the fireplace while Lara felt inside the panel with her hand. She could not feel anything there and moved over to where the two boys had found a small hole in the side.

Rufus shoved his hand into the hole and pulled out a box identical to the one found inside the castle tower, with the same gold initials, *JCK*.

"It's the real clue," cried Rufus, holding up the box.

"Let's keep this to ourselves for now," said Lara. "Uncle Herb looked so upset last time, let's not tell him in case it leads to another dead end."

Before they had a chance to open the precious box, they heard voices and footsteps outside.

"It's Dad," whispered Tom. "I'll distract them—get everything back to how it was."

Tom darted outside leaving Rufus and Lara frantically trying to move the stone back to its original space. They shoved the stone and tried to feel inside for a switch or lever, all the while hearing the footsteps coming closer and closer with Tom chattering nervously to try to distract them.

"It won't budge," said Rufus, looking around for another kind of switch on the fireplace.

Suddenly steps were heard right outside the door. Lara jumped up to replace the painting on the wall. Her fingers searched for a switch inside the panel in vain. The door handle was turning, Lara shoved the panel in frustration, releasing a spring which sprung the panel back in its place and the stone back across the fireplace with a loud thud. As quick as lighting Lara slammed the painting on the wall and turned to face the door just as it was opening.

"What have you been doing in here, crashing about?" said Mr Burt, with Tom standing behind him looking very relieved.

"We were playing pirate shipwrecks," said Rufus. He picked up a chair and crashed it loudly on the stone floor. "See?"

"Pick that up you *stupid* boy, before you get me barred from this place," said Mr Burt, looking over his shoulder with genuine concern. "I'm going back home, and you'd best come with me, tea will be ready soon, and it's getting late."

Annoyingly, nobody could speak a word about their discovery during the ride up the hill home as they sat piled into the front of Mr Burt's old rusty truck. Lara noticed Rufus shifting uncomfortably and saw an odd-shaped bulge in his stomach where he had hidden the box. Luckily Mr Burt's eyes were fixed straight ahead, and he did not pay any attention to them.

After what seemed like an age, the truck came to a stop in front of the bridge, and all three jumped out and pelted towards the kitchen.

They stopped in their tracks suddenly inside, their eyes widening in horror. At the table, Great-Uncle Herb was sharing a cup of tea with Mr Bunce and Karim.

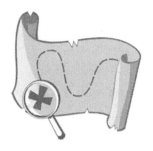

Chapter 16
The Second Box

They were stunned, not just by the presence of the two visitors but by Uncle Herb's relaxed appearance. Tom and Lara stared in disbelief, while Rufus' arm was involuntarily raised to point at Mr Bunce and Karim.

"What… are *they* doing here?" he spluttered.

At that moment, Mr Burt followed them through the door and raised his eyebrows in confusion. Mrs Burt busied herself with the teapot.

"Good news," said Uncle Herb, his eyes not meeting anyone else's in the room. "The police called me, and the thieves have been arrested."

"Well what are they doing here then?" asked Rufus, becoming very conscious of the secret box hidden underneath his coat.

Uncle Herb chuckled nervously. "Very funny, boy. The thieves were three men in the area, who were responsible for three other burglaries of artwork in the past few weeks. The painting will be returned in the next few days." He stared at Rufus in a silent plea to stop questioning him.

"Very fortuitous I'm sure, Mr Kexley," said Mr Bunce, rubbing and wringing his hands together on the table. "Very remarkable indeed, that such an incident should occur hours after we viewed the painting."

"Yes, it is, isn't it?" remarked Lara in a rather sarcastic tone. "Surely you don't expect us to fall for that trick?"

"I received a call from Cornwall's constabulary directly," said Uncle Herb, whose voice was becoming angry and his face reddening. "Mr Bunce has come here to discuss some financial matters with me, and it's not a conversation for silly children to take part in. Now get out." He waved a hand, dismissing them.

Mrs Burt turned, looking concerned. "Why don't you go upstairs, eh kids?" she said, motioning towards the door with her eyes. "I'll get you some nice dinner later once your great-uncle has finished with these two gentlemen."

Lara stormed out, while Rufus was still frozen to the spot and had to be nudged out by Tom.

Once they were in the large hallway out of earshot of the kitchen, next to the tall Egyptian statues in the hallway, they let out their shock and surprise.

"What on *earth* is Uncle Herb doing," exclaimed Lara.

"He's completely lost it," said Rufus, rubbing his head. "Stark-raving mad."

"Let's get out of here where we can talk properly," said Tom. "You never know when they're going to sneak up on us in here. Let's take Barney down to the beach and have a look at the box."

"That other old weirdo Sam snoops on us down there," said Rufus.

"Sam's harmless," said Tom, "and he doesn't talk to anyone in the village anyway. It's better than staying here. Let's go."

Lara and Rufus followed Tom through a side door to the back of the castle to avoid going back through the kitchen. It was almost five o'clock, and the air was still warm and breezy. The tide was coming in, and waves stretched out back and forth across the golden sand. They were glad to find the beach empty, although Barney ran to the big rock where Sam had previously perched and sniffed alongside it, as if looking for traces of his friend.

They sat down on the warm, soft sand, close to the cliff path where they could not be seen from the castle windows. Rufus took out the small box and felt the familiar JCK initials with his fingers before unclasping the box. The inside of the box was identical to the first, with purple silk lining and a folded piece of paper. Rufus took a deep breath, hoping not to find more dried up tobacco inside. He cautiously unfolded the paper, his heart leaping as he read the words on the page aloud:

John Crispian Kexley, Jack be my name

I travelled, prospered, won riches and fame,

My greatest discovery, yours to find

If you would follow the path of my mind.

Where the weeping willow hangs its sad boughs

Lies my faithful friend, whose remembrance endows

Words that will guide you past his resting place

To begin a journey— begin the race.

They paused, each desperately trying to discover the meaning of the words written by Captain Jack Crispian Kexley. It sounded remarkably exciting, but did not seem to guide them anywhere. Lara wondered about the 'friend' mentioned in the lines, whilst Tom thought about the race. Rufus pictured images of 'riches and fame' and imagined himself finding the treasure and appearing in newspapers.

"It doesn't mean much, does it?" said Rufus after a few moments.

"Poetry always means *something*," replied Lara.

"What does it mean then, boffin?" sneered Rufus.

"Well you have to look at it line by line," said Lara, frowning at the lines on the page as she thought deeply. "The first two lines are pretty obvious—we already knew his name and that he was rich and famous. The next bit... 'path of my mind'... I guess he's telling us that we need to think the same way as he does to follow what he's thinking. Then 'boughs'—what are boughs?"

"Tree branches," said Tom, who, like his father, was a keen gardener and took an interest in all aspects of natural life.

"Ok, so we have to look under willow tree branches, for his 'friend'... who will give us words to the next clue. He talks about 'remembrance' and 'resting place' so his friend is obviously dead..."

"A grave," said Rufus. "So, we have to look for a grave under a willow tree, the grave of Jack's friend. Where's the nearest graveyard, Tom?"

"There's one in the village; there's willow trees there but the Kexley graves aren't underneath it, they're in a separate family tomb right in the middle of the graveyard."

"Well, if it's a friend they're probably not related," said Lara. "We should check it out."

"And what does the 'race' part mean?" asked Tom.

"I don't know… race to find the treasure maybe… I can see your mum at the top of the cliff," said Rufus, hastily shoving the box back into his coat and the paper into his pocket. "She's waving at us, we'd better go back up."

Barney ran up the cliff path to greet Mrs Burt, who he hoped had some food for him. Lara, Rufus and Tom followed.

"Your uncle's taken the two gentlemen back into his office," said Mrs Burt. "I've baked a nice shepherd's pie for you all, come back to the kitchen. I've got some meat for young Barney here too."

Barney barked in delight, as if understanding Mrs Burt's words.

"Why did Herb let those two men back in, Mum?" asked Tom, as they walked back towards the kitchen. "I don't trust them, and I didn't think that Herb did either."

"Your dad and I don't like them, but we believe they've offered him some kind of business deal or money. And crikey, how much we need it at the moment! I've made up some beds in the other part of the castle, so they won't be near Lara and Rufus."

"They're staying *here*?" said Lara, looking incredulous.

"Yes, unfortunately," said Mrs Burt. "Just stay out of their way, and don't upset your uncle. He's got a lot on his plate at the moment, and the business needs all the financial help we can get."

Rufus opened his mouth to object, and Tom shot him a look that hinted he should say no more. Tom knew from personal experience that it was not worth arguing with Herb, however much you disagreed with him. He also knew that his father and Herb's organic plant business had suffered over the past few years. Tom loved living at the castle and having the vast grounds, greenhouses and private beach to roam around in. He felt that it more than made up for the lack of holidays, video games, electronics and fancy shoes and clothes that his classmates boasted of. As much as he disliked the idea of Mr Bunce and Karim staying at the castle and working on some kind of deal with Herb, if it meant a delay before the bank would seize the castle then he could understand Herb's motivation. He only hoped that he would be able to find the treasure with his two new friends before the others did, to make life better for everyone at the castle as well as for Lara and Rufus too.

"Cheer up," said Lara to Tom, who had noticed the apprehensive look on his face and that he was hanging back slightly from Mrs Burt and Rufus. "We know more

than they do, and we'll be back on the hunt first thing
tomorrow."

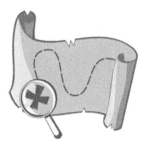

Chapter 17
Making Plans

Mrs Burt had prepared another appetising dinner that evening. The shepherd's pie was delicious, served with roasted vegetables and warm freshly baked bread with creamy butter.

Once again Rufus seemed to consume the entire meal at lightning speed, before eagerly passing his plate to Mrs Burt for seconds. Just when he thought he was so stuffed he couldn't eat another bite, Mrs Burt brought a warm, thick chocolate pudding out of the oven, the mouth-watering smell filling the kitchen immediately.

"I'll have some of that, Mrs B," he said, rubbing his stomach as if to free up some room.

"I don't know how you eat so much and stay so little," observed Lara, who had been passing small handfuls of mincemeat to Barney, who gratefully licked her hands under the table. "It's as if there's a fat person trapped inside a skinny boy's body."

"I don't know how you talk so much and stay so boring," quipped Rufus. "It's as if there's an old long-winded person trapped inside a kid's body." Mrs Burt had gone out of the kitchen door to collect the dry washing from the line, and Tom seized the opportunity to change the subject before another argument erupted between the two cousins.

"We're probably not going to get to the graveyard tonight," said Tom. "How early can you be up tomorrow? I think it's best if we leave before Bunce and Karim are awake and poking about in our business."

"Well I can get up at any time, Lara will be too busy snoring," said Rufus, pouring cream on his dessert.

"Very funny, not," she said. "I can get up. What time does the sun come up?"

"About five o'clock," said Tom. "How about I meet you at five-thirty by the front entrance gates?"

"Fine, we'll be there," said Lara.

"You'd better take the box and clue with you, Tom," said Rufus. "With Bunce and Karim here, you never know when they're going to come snooping."

Rufus put the note of paper back inside the box and handed it to Tom, who placed it in his pocket. Lara looked up just after the box had been concealed and gasped, seeing Karim's face at the glass panel of the kitchen door that led to the hallway. He quickly swung the door open and stepped inside to three startled faces.

"Er, hello, I just came in to get some water," he said.

There was an awkward pause of a few moments.

"There's some glasses in the cupboard over the sink," replied Tom.

"Right," said Karim, shuffling towards the sink, taking what seemed like a long time to look at each glass in the cupboard before selecting one.

"What was that shop you said we should go to tomorrow?" asked Lara, winking at the two boys behind Karim's back. "I really would like to buy a postcard and some fudge for my friend Daisy."

"The post office has loads of postcards, and they sell some fudge as well," responded Tom, following Lara's lead. "After we can go to the yacht club and take a look at the boats. Maybe we can go out with one of the fishermen."

"Anywhere I can buy a fishing rod?" asked Rufus.

"Yeah, there's a place at the yacht club that sells fishing tackle and hires out …"

Finally, Karim had exited through the kitchen door and shut it behind him. They sighed and sank back into their chairs.

"What a nuisance," said Lara in a whisper, in case Karim was still lingering in the corridor. "I suppose he saw you two handing over the box and has probably seen the identical one that we found before with Uncle Herb and will now go and tell Bunce all about it." She glared at the window as if Karim was still standing on the other side. "I wanted him to think we weren't doing anything important tomorrow just in case he decides to follow us. That would be so annoying now that we've got a lead to go on."

"I still think it's safer for me to hang on to the box for now, with those two staying here," said Tom. "I'm not sure if he really believed our fudge and fishing plans, but hopefully since we're leaving so early, he'll still be asleep."

After they had finished their pudding, Tom left with his mother to walk back to their cottage near the front gates. Lara, Rufus and Barney headed upstairs to their rooms. They were all tired from the day's activities and had a very early start ahead of them the next day.

Chapter 18
An Early Start

The following morning Lara woke up to a soft knocking on her door. The sun was already streaming through the curtains, and she stretched her legs.

"It's five," whispered Rufus. "Hurry *up*."

Lara quickly washed and tiptoed towards the kitchen with Rufus and Barney. Suddenly they heard a voice coming from Uncle Herb's bedroom.

"What do you think you're doing, you snivelling weasel?"

Lara and Rufus froze in their tracks and glanced up in surprise.

"Give me back my sword you festering pile of snot," continued Uncle Herb.

Rufus raised his eyebrows in confusion and pushed the door which was slightly ajar. He saw his uncle tossing and turning in his bed.

"You'll never take this onion. Never," Uncle Herb yelled while flailing his arms.

Rufus moved his head back out of the room.

"He's talking in his sleep," whispered Rufus, stifling a giggle. "Funny sort of dream he must be having."

Rufus and Lara continued to the kitchen where Lara opened a tin of dog food for Barney and filled up his water bowl. A few minutes later they moved quickly across the bridge and driveway to where Tom stood waiting for them at the gates. They headed down the hill towards the village which was already coming to life. Fishermen were preparing their boats to go out to sea, the milkman was delivering milk and orange juice to each door and the postman cycled by on his bike. Each person smiled and waved as they passed.

Tom led Lara and Rufus past the post office and The Laughing Pig towards a small, grey stone church. They followed a footpath around the side of the building into a large graveyard.

"There's the Kexley tomb," said Tom, pointing to a large rectangular structure in the middle of the graveyard. It was bright white and had figures carved into the stone at the top that were looking up into the sky.

"Cool," said Rufus, his eyes widening with glee. "It looks like the tomb in my computer game *Corpses Attack* where the flesh-eating zombies all come out at night and kill everyone."

"Trust you to enjoy something like that," said Lara with a shudder.

They moved closer to the tomb and saw a list of names engraved at the front. They scanned the list until they saw *John Crispian Kexley – 1832 – 1901*.

"You don't suppose the treasure is buried in the tomb, do you?" asked Lara, sounding hopeful. "After all, Egyptians buried their treasure in tombs, and Captain Kexley might've got the idea from his travels."

"No, it's not there," said Tom. "A few years ago, the tomb was opened, plus other Kexleys have been buried here since the captain died, so they would have spotted it. Maybe we should try that willow tree over there."

They walked over to a willow tree in the corner of the graveyard, where a single grave stood underneath. Straight away they knew that it could not be the right one, as it was made of a shiny black stone that did not look very old. The front of the gravestone read *Maureen Philpot, 1930 – 2014*.

"What do we do now?" asked Rufus, who was feeling restless.

"We've got to find out who the friend was," said Lara. "Maybe there's a book about him in the library, we should go there."

"It will be closed, silly," scoffed Rufus. "It's half-past six. Do you have a computer at your place, Tom? Maybe we can search the internet for Captain Jack Kexley."

"Yeah, I do; let's go back and get breakfast first though, I'm starving."

The three of them, followed by Barney, walked back through the village up the winding hill towards the castle. By the time they got back to the kitchen Mrs Burt had most of the breakfast on the table, and to their dismay, Karim and Mr Bunce were already seated. Barney growled at them, making the pair jump up in fright, until Lara gently stroked his head and told him to be quiet.

"I don't believe I have had the pleasure of a formal introduction," said Mr Bunce, smirking in a way that implied interacting with the three was anything but pleasurable. He held out his hand then hastily withdrew it, frightened that Barney might snap it off.

"Reginald Bunce," he said, attempting to recover his composure. "I am a collector of antiquities and a visiting historian at the British Museum. I specialise in ancient world history and have made a study of its relics. I am writing an editorial on circumnavigation and your ancestor, Captain John Kexley, came up as part of my research." He paused after this long introduction and added as an afterthought, "Oh, and this is Karim. He's an intern from Cairo University."

Karim nodded hello.

"This is my son, Tom," said Mrs Burt, noting that he was unlikely to introduce himself, "and Herb's great-nephew and niece, Rufus and Lara."

Rufus and Lara seated themselves as far away as possible from Mr Bunce and Karim, whilst Tom helped his mother bring the rest of the food to the table.

"I would be happy to answer any of your questions on Egyptian history, children, as I'm sure you have never before met any world-renowned experts on Egyptology."

"I have a question, Mr Bunce," said Lara. Having attended many of her mother's events and lectures at the university, she was already well-versed in Egyptology, but she decided to have some fun. "Who followed Seti the First to the throne?"

"Er, well, that's an interesting question," Mr Bunce stumbled.

"But not a difficult one, is it?" said Lara.

Mr Bunce's face turned several shades of pink.

"Ramesses the Second," answered Karim quietly.

"I *knew* that Karim," blasted Mr Bunce. "There is no need for you to speak on my behalf." He folded his arms and stuck his nose high in the air, blinking rapidly.

"And who was Ramesses the Second's mother, Mr Bunce?" continued Lara, enjoying herself.

"Well, I say, give me a moment…" Mr Bunce spluttered. His cheeks were now turning to the colour of ripe tomatoes. Karim opened his mouth to answer and closed it upon receiving a murderous glance from Mr Bunce.

"Ok, I think we've had enough questions and answers," said Mrs Burt with a nervous laugh, who was feeling almost as uncomfortable as Mr Bunce. "Anyone for sausages?"

Breakfast passed awkwardly, with most of the conversation being between Mr Bunce and Mrs Burt, the latter trying valiantly to lighten the heavy atmosphere. Karim was paying keen attention to Lara, Rufus and Tom, looking up with interest every time they said something to one another, which they found rather tiresome.

Mr Burt walked in towards the end of breakfast.

"There you are, Tom," he said. "I've been looking all over for you. I need you in the greenhouses; we've had a very good order come in for plants, and the new packaging has arrived. I need your help packing up the orders."

"But Dad, I was going to go out with Lara and Rufus this morning," protested Tom, dismayed.

"I'm sorry Tom, I don't think I can do it on my own, we really need to fulfil this order today." Mr Burt felt guilty about asking for his son's help when he was with friends, as Tom had rarely brought any friends home from school and spent a lot of time helping out. Unfortunately, they had been waiting a long time for a good order to come through and needed it to be ready in the next few hours.

"Ok," conceded Tom, rising to get up.

"The house is unlocked," he whispered to Lara and Rufus in a very low voice. "You can just go into my room and use the computer, there's no password."

"We can help you with the order," said Rufus, in a louder voice. "Just show us what to do." Rufus surprised Lara as well as himself. He had never volunteered to do work before. Indeed, he spent most of his time at school scheming new ways to avoid doing any work.

"Oh, alright," said Mr Burt, pleased at having two additional volunteers, although a little uncertain of the mischievous-looking Rufus. "Many hands make light work."

They followed Mr Burt out of the kitchen to the side of the castle. Barney followed close behind. Walking away from the beach, they followed a path to the back of the castle that led to Uncle Herb and Mr Burt's business on the other side. There was a large greenhouse surrounded by vegetable patches.

"Thanks for offering to help," said Tom, who was unused to working with anyone other than his parents and Herb. "You didn't have to do that." He smiled at the two cousins and reflected on how much he was enjoying having them around. They already felt like his friends.

"Well it's more fun to search for the next clue with you," said Lara.

"And it beats spending the morning being snooped on by Karim," added Rufus. "This way hopefully he leaves us alone and goes off somewhere else."

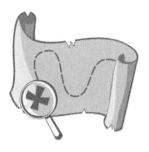

Chapter 19
Searching for a Faithful Friend

Time passed quickly as the three busily packed the plants and vegetables into the boxes. Mr Burt sealed the containers and took them to his truck. About halfway through, he opened a box packed by Rufus and frowned.

"What the devil is this?" he bellowed. Staring back at him on top of the order was a smiley face made out of tomatoes for eyes, a carrot for a nose, a runner bean smile and cauliflower hair. "Is this why you're taking twice as long as the others to pack boxes?"

"Just sprucing it up a bit," said Rufus. "I think they're going to like it and order more from you now."

"Humph! Well, I don't have time to unpack and remove all this foolishness, but cut it out, you daft boy."

Tom and Lara giggled until they looked up and saw Karim walking past for the fifth time that morning.

"I wish he'd stop creeping up on us like this," Lara whispered to Tom. "It's getting really annoying."

A few minutes later Uncle Herb walked past, followed by Mr Bunce, who was talking nonstop. Uncle Herb looked as if he was trying to get away.

Finally, the last box was loaded into the truck, and Mrs Burt came in with lunch bags.

"Here, I thought I'd bring you some sandwiches seeing as your uncle is having lunch with the two visitors."

"Thanks Mrs B, you're an old dear," said Rufus, sounding like his grandad.

"Less of the old, thank you," said Mrs Burt, laughing. "Seriously though, you should all try to be a bit friendlier to Mr Bunce and… what *is* the other fellow's name?"

"Karim, an *intern* from Cairo University," said Rufus, mimicking Mr Bunce's pompous voice and manner, by placing his hands on his hips and sticking his small belly out as far as possible.

"Alright, alright," said Mrs Burt, trying not to laugh and failing. "Well if you can't be nice to them then at least try to stay out of their way, and your uncle's! He's had a face like thunder this morning."

They checked that Karim was nowhere to be seen, then crossed the lawn in front of the house, down towards the beach. Tom unpacked the sandwiches whilst

Lara poured some water into a plastic bowl for Barney and gave him some chicken Mrs Burt had wrapped in foil. Barney had run over towards Sam who was perched in his usual spot on the rock. The old man chuckled joyously at being licked and tickled by the friendly dog.

"Do you think we should ask him about the friend?" said Lara, in a whisper so quiet that Rufus and Tom struggled to hear her.

"Ask me what, child," yelled Sam, still chuckling whilst patting Barney's silky fur.

"He must have incredible hearing," said Lara, amazed.

"Wow, *nothing* gets past you does it," said Rufus, rolling his eyes.

Lara frowned.

"Well we might as well ask him now," she said.

"Ask me *what*, cretins," said Sam, his quick temper starting to flare again.

"Well if you must know, we need to know who Captain John Kexley's friends were," said Lara. "We need to know who his *best* friend was."

"Pah. Foolish children. He didn't have any friends. He was a notorious gamester and lost friends as soon as he tricked money from them, which was all the time."

"Well he must have had friends," protested Lara, "he wrote -"

"Lots of party invitations," chimed in Rufus, glaring at his cousin for nearly giving away their secret. "The man was a party animal."

"Nonsense," snapped Sam. "His wife Jane took care of any social events, and Captain Kexley rarely turned up. He spent most of his time with his horse."

"His horse?" repeated Tom, a vague idea forming in his mind. "Was it a *racehorse*?"

"Why ask when you know the answer already," said Sam with disdain.

"What was the racehorse's name?" Tom continued.

"What am I, a talking encyclopaedia? Leave me alone. Except for the dog," he added, on reflexion. "He can stay."

Rufus and Lara wanted to know what idea had sprung in Tom's mind, but did not dare to broach the subject again in front of Sam with his sharp hearing. They wolfed down their sandwiches, anxious to move away from the beach where they could discuss matters privately.

"Let's go to my house," said Tom, finishing the last sandwich. Lara had to call Barney three times before he would move away from Sam, where he laid with his head on Sam's knee.

"It *is* maddening how you run to Sam all the time Barney," said Lara, when they reached the top of the cliff path. "He's not very nice to us, yet you always jump all over him as if he's your best mate and the one who feeds you and lets you jump on their bed at night."

Barney jumped up and put his two front paws around Lara's leg, panting and holding on tightly as she tried to walk. It was as if he wanted to assure her that she was still his best friend.

"Alright, alright," she said laughing, patting Barney's head and moving his paws. "Tell us what you were thinking about the racehorse, Tom."

"The rhyme Captain Kexley wrote talked about a race at the end—'begin the race'—his faithful friend was his *horse.*"

"I think you're right," exclaimed Rufus. "Let's go to your computer and see if we can find out what his horse was called and where he was buried."

Tom heard a noise coming from behind him. He stopped in his tracks and Barney ran up to a large gorse bush, sniffing it with fervour.

"Did one of you just sneeze?" he asked.

"Not me… Barney come back over here," Lara called. Tom shrugged, and they continued towards his cottage. Inside, the door opened to a small lounge, with flowery wallpaper and very basic furnishings.

"Come on, my room is over here," said Tom, blushing as he tried to usher Lara away from the family pictures she had noticed on the fireplace.

"Hey look what you're wearing in this one," said Lara, spotting a picture of Tom dressed as Frankenstein's monster for Halloween.

"And this one is hilarious," cried Rufus, laughing at a toddler picture of Tom. "Look at that bird outfit. Brilliant!"

"We don't have time for that," insisted Tom, pushing the two cousins away from the fireplace, whilst hastily shoving the frame behind the rubbish bin when their backs were turned.

"Alright, alright," said Rufus. "Keep your beak on."

Tom groaned as Lara and Rufus could not contain their laughter.

"That outfit is egg-cellent," said Lara.

"Don't tease him, Lara, it's getting *hawkward*," added Rufus.

"Enough already," cried Tom, desperately wanting to change the subject.

"Ok," said Rufus, in a solemn tone. "You *wing*."

Tom looked sternly at his two friends.

"That's enough you guys," he said, before a wide grin spread on his face. "Give it a *nest*."

They giggled so much at their silliness that they quite forgot what they were doing. Barney loved when they were happy and jumped around them, wagging his tail excitedly.

"Oh yeah, the horse," remembered Tom after a few moments. "Come on, my computer's over here."

Rufus and Lara sat on the bed as Tom turned on his ancient PC tower. The computer slowly whirred into life, releasing a number of fizzes and bangs as the gigantic tube monitor displayed a background picture of the Burts standing outside the castle. Lara could not help noticing that other than the computer, there were no frills either in Tom's room or the whole house. The television in the living room was very small, and Tom's bed was furnished with a homemade patchwork quilt. There were a few posters of animals and nature photos dotted around the room, covering up the peeling of the wallpaper. There was also a collection of plants on the windowsill that Tom had grown from seeds.

"Ok, let's try… Captain John Kexley's racehorse," said Tom, typing the words into a search engine.

The children waited anxiously while the slow browser loaded the page.

"It's just this month's sports results," said Tom. "Let's try something else… John Kexley, horse."

The page took even longer to load.

"This computer's even worse than Grandma's. Maybe you should sell it to Bunce," joked Rufus. "He collects antiques."

Lara dug Rufus in the ribs and scowled at him for his rudeness. She sensed that the Burts' lack of money may be a sore subject for Tom.

"Oomph," Rufus groaned.

"It's coming," said Tom. "Ok, no good… nothing," he thought aloud, scrolling down the page. "Here's something, 'pictured left are John Kexley and his horse, Lord Anthony'."

"Click on that," said Lara whilst jumping up to get a better view of the screen.

The page slowly loaded to an article with the heading *Cornish Horseracing in the 19th and 20th Century*. Tom quickly scanned the information on the page until he saw the picture of Captain John Kexley standing next to a fine black thoroughbred racehorse. John Kexley wore a grey suit and was holding a trophy. Tom read the text next to the picture:

Pictured left are John Kexley and his horse—Lord Anthony. Kexley trained Lord Anthony and entered him into his first race at Polwellan racetrack in 1856. Lord Anthony finished in second place and went on to compete in races across the country over the next nine years. Kexley often travelled to watch the races, and after Lord Anthony retired from professional racing, he lived at Kexley's estate in Cornwall. Lord Anthony's remains were buried at Polwellan racetrack in 1877.

"Begin the race, it makes sense now," said Lara. "The next clue is at Lord Anthony's grave, at the racetrack. Do you know where it is, Tom?"

"Polwellan isn't far from here," said Tom, "I'm pretty sure they don't have races there anymore though. Let's search for it next."

Over the next few minutes the children discovered that the Polwellan racetrack had closed in the 1970s, but upon searching through maps and aerial pictures, it looked as though the track was still there.

"Looks like Polwellan is nearly three miles away," said Lara, "is there a bus that goes there?"

"It would take forever," explained Tom. "We'd have to get a bus into a bigger town then wait for an hourly bus that goes through all the villages. It would be quickest to go by bike, I have one—you can rent yours from the village. Would Barney be able to keep up with us?"

"Yeah, he'd love it," said Lara, "as long as we don't go too fast and stop so he can drink water." Barney woofed in agreement and jumped on Tom's bed laying his front paws over Lara's legs.

"We should go tomorrow, so we have longer in the day," suggested Rufus. "Should we get up early again like we did today?"

"You won't be able to rent bikes until nine o'clock," said Tom. "Why don't we go to get the bikes when the shop opens and take our lunch with us?"

"I can't wait, this is so exciting," Lara exclaimed. "Do you think the clue will lead us to the treasure there or somewhere in the castle?"

"Well I reckon the curse has always been about the castle," said Rufus, "it must be somewhere here. Have you ever done a proper search of the place Tom? There must be loads of secret passageways."

"I know one of the secret passageways, but I reckon there's more."

"Really? The castle has secret passages? Can you show us this afternoon?" asked Lara.

"Ok," said Tom, "don't expect anything too exciting though, they're just dark, narrow corridors really."

At that moment the children heard the front door open and jumped. They heard two sets of footsteps as Mrs Burt walked into Tom's bedroom, followed by Karim.

"Hello children, I didn't expect to find you here," said Mrs Burt, who rarely saw her son indoors at all during the daytime. "Karim would like to use your computer, Tom, his phone signal is down, and he wants to write an email to his parents in Cairo."

They looked at each other, all sharing the same suspicion. Karim must have been outside snooping when he sneezed somewhere near the gorse bush.

"Er, we're a bit busy at the moment, can you come back later?" asked Tom.

"Certainly not," answered Mrs Burt. "Karim is our guest."

"Let me just do something quick, won't be a minute Mrs B," said Rufus, who went over to the computer and tried to block the screen with his back as he took hold of the mouse.

Lara sensed Rufus was trying to do something and that she needed to distract Karim from the screen. With only a split second to think, she pointed to the window and screamed.

"There's a *giant* mongoose outside," she cried.

Despite Lara's ludicrous claim, the distraction worked, and both Mrs Burt and Karim jumped towards the window.

"There's nothing there," said Mrs Burt, squinting her eyes. "Honestly, I don't know what's got into you kids today."

Rufus closed the internet screen, and the three stood up to leave.

"Thank you, I really appreciate it," said Karim, looking uncomfortable as the children left the room and quickly headed back towards the castle.

"Nice distraction Lara," said Rufus. "You could have come up with something better though. "A *mongoose*?"

"Well, I had to think of something. What were you doing anyway?"

"Deleting all of the browser history," Rufus replied with a grin. "Now if he tries to search for the pages we looked at he won't be able to."

"Nice," said Tom. "Lara's right though, we do need to be more careful."

Chapter 20
The Secret Passage

A few minutes later the children were back in the entrance hallway with its black and white chequered floor and two large Egyptian statues.

"So where do we go to find the secret passage?" asked Lara.

"In the library," said Tom.

After taking a torch from the kitchen, Tom led Lara, Rufus and Barney up a staircase through the portrait gallery, then into another long corridor. He opened a large wooden arched door into an expansive room filled floor to ceiling with rows and rows of books. The room had a very musty smell. Rufus sneezed profusely as they looked around.

"You alright, mate?" asked Tom, giving Rufus a large pat on the back.

"He's pretty allergic to dust and stuff like that," said Lara, answering for her cousin who was still sneezing.

"Every superhero has their… ach-oooo… kryptonite," spluttered Rufus between sneezes. "Hurry up and get us to the passage."

Tom got on his hands and knees and crawled under a table in the middle of the library. Lara and Rufus looked at each other in surprise.

"The secret passage starts from under there?" asked Lara, watching Tom search around the inside of the table with his hands.

"No, there's a switch under here that pulls one of the books out… ah, got it."

With a quiet clicking sound, a book shot out from the bookcase about two inches. Tom turned the book, which appeared to be attached to the wall, at a 180-degree angle and pushed it back into place. Suddenly the entire column of shelves sprang towards him, revealing an opening and stairs leading downwards. He turned on his torch and motioned for Lara, Rufus and Barney to go ahead of him.

"Be quiet as we go through," he said. "There's parts of this passage where people can hear us from outside, and Herb doesn't like anyone using the passage."

Lara stroked Barney's head and whispered to him to be quiet. He licked her hand then started sniffing the stairs. Tom carefully closed the doorway behind them then followed Barney down the stairs with his torch.

The passage got progressively narrower as they moved down the steps, which made Rufus and Lara feel as if they were being closed in.

"It's alright," whispered Tom, guessing their thoughts, "it opens up in a bit."

Soon the steps stopped, and the passage did indeed open up, coming to a fork. "Left is towards the study, right is towards the kitchen," explained Tom, still in a whisper. "They're both blocked so you can't go right the way through. Let's go left."

They continued. After a few feet, Barney heard voices with his sharp ears. They were voices he knew, and one was a voice he did not like at all. He bared his teeth but did not make a sound as he knew that Lara wanted him to be quiet. The three stopped and listened.

"It's Bunce," whispered Rufus. "I think I can hear Herb as well."

Lara, Rufus and Tom tiptoed closer until the voices became loud enough to make out the words.

"It's a good offer, Mr Kexley," said Mr Bunce. Even though the children could not see him, Lara pictured Mr Bunce's greasy appearance and shuddered.

"You said you only needed a few days for your... *study*," replied Uncle Herb.

"Mr Kexley, we are already paying you five times the cost of a decent hotel... I'll double it."

"Why are you so eager to stay here?"

"We are making some good progress in research for my editorial, and it helps to be in Captain Kexley's abode to feel close to the man."

"Right..." responded Uncle Herb, not sounding convinced. "How much longer are we talking?"

"Let's start with a week," said Mr Bunce.

"Fine."

Rufus' nose was starting to feel incredibly itchy again. He smothered his face with his hand and held his breath for a few seconds. It was no good.

"*Achooo.*" Rufus' sneeze exploded out of him and reverberated loudly around the secret passage.

"Bless you?" said Uncle Herb, though he was unsure who he was saying it to.

"Karim, use a handkerchief if you please," scolded Mr Bunce. "Disgusting manners."

"What?" said Karim sounding confused.

After Mr Bunce apologised on Karim's behalf, a long silence followed, and Tom was not sure if the men had left the room. They continued down the passage until they came to a dead end.

"So, Mr Bunce is paying Uncle Herb a lot of money to stay here," whispered Lara.

"No surprise there," said Rufus. "Herb doesn't like him any more than we do, but he's desperate."

"If they want to stay longer it's because they think they're onto something," said Tom. "I bet Karim has been reporting everything we do back to Bunce and is going to keep spying on us."

"How can we stop him?" asked Lara. "The last thing we want is him following us to the racetrack tomorrow."

The three were silent for a few moments in thought.

"Do you think we should tell Uncle Herb what has been going on?" suggested Lara. "Maybe if he realises that we have another clue, he won't let them stay here anymore."

"It's too much of a risk," replied Tom. "I don't think he really believes we can find the treasure, and he could decide to sell the clues to them or something like that, to make more money."

The thought of Mr Bunce getting his sweaty hands on the next clue was not an attractive one.

They turned and made their way back into the library, carefully making sure that the books and switch for opening the secret door were returned to how they had previously appeared.

"Which rooms are Bunce and Karim staying in?" asked Rufus.

"Further down the corridor from Herb's study; there's two bedrooms with a bathroom in between," said Tom. "Why do you ask?"

"Just because they're staying here, doesn't mean they have to *enjoy* their stay," replied Rufus with a smirk on his face.

"Don't do anything stupid," said Lara. "I can't stand them either, especially Bunce, but if you trash their rooms or something, it will just make Uncle Herb angry, and Tom's mum will have to clean it up."

"Don't worry about that," said Rufus, looking distant.

"Ok…" said Tom, wondering what on earth Rufus was planning. "Are you going now?"

"Yes, before they go back to their rooms."

"Want us to come with you?" asked Lara, who was also intrigued.

"No, best not. Karim will be looking for us again soon, and if he sees you two somewhere else, he can't follow all of us."

Chapter 21
Rufus Gets to Work

"Lara, Rufus…" called Mrs Burt. "Oh, there you are," she said, seeing Lara standing with Tom outside the kitchen. "Come quickly, your grandad's on the phone."

Lara rushed inside and picked up the receiver.

"Grandad?"

"Lara, how are you? We've just docked for the day, I can't talk for long, I'm calling on my mobile."

"Oh, right, er, we're ok Grandad," said Lara. "How's the cruise?"

"Splendid, splendid, although Grandma doesn't like the entertainment, she says it's a budget rip-off of *Strictly Come Dancing*. How's the castle?"

"It's ok," said Lara.

"Now listen, I know I warned you before, but please tell me Rufus is not trying to break into the south-west tower. I know what he's like and it's been bothering me."

"Er no, we're not going to *break* in…" said Lara, choosing her words carefully. Grandad sighed on the other end of the phone.

"It really is dangerous," he said. "Not many people know this, Lara, but one of our cousins had a terrible accident in that tower. He lived in the village, and we used to play in there as boys. Herb was away at school, he got a scholarship, was always cleverer than the rest of us. Anyway, my cousin got concussion after falling, and he lost his eyesight, poor fellow. Turned a bit funny after that, angry all the time at everyone."

Lara froze, unable to speak as realisation dawned.

"Anyway" continued Grandad, I'm glad you're all ok, it was on my mind, that's all. I'd better go now, Grandma is calling me over. Take care, Lara."

"Bye Grandad."

As Lara hung up the phone, she felt a pang of compassion for Sam. Everything fell into place, his knowledge of the family history, his anger, even his insistent belief in the castle's curse. She considered whether to tell Rufus, the Burts and even her uncle— and decided against it. Everyone knew the tower was dangerous—she herself had come close to stumbling, as she recalled with a shiver. Sam had not wanted to discuss it with them. Maybe if they found the treasure Uncle Herb would have enough money to repair the tower and make it safe again. Lara tried to put the past tragedy out of her mind and went to find Tom.

Meanwhile, Rufus had collected a few things from his bedroom and headed quickly towards the bedrooms past the study. Most of the doors were locked; he peered through the keyhole of one and saw that all the furniture had been covered in white dust sheets. Like a lot of the castle, it looked like it was asleep, waiting to be woken up and brought back to life again.

Rufus hurried along and finally found a door slightly ajar. After checking through the keyhole to make sure that nobody was inside, he hurried inside. The room was neat and tidy, and the bed had been made. A jacket was hung up on the back of the door and looked too modern and slim to fit Mr Bunce. Rufus realised he was standing in Karim's bedroom.

The room was small and consisted of a single bed, wardrobe and a desk by the window. Rufus moved over to the desk. There were a few papers neatly stacked and a textbook with Egyptian drawings on the front. Lara's mother had once explained to Rufus that these were called hieroglyphics and were found inside tombs where kings, queens and other important people were buried. Next to the books was a photograph. It looked old, the paper was thick, and the clothes looked slightly old-fashioned. It showed a young boy sitting on a man's shoulders with the Great Pyramid of Giza in the background.

That must be Karim and his dad, thought Rufus. Suddenly it did not feel right to mess around in Karim's room, and he crept back into the corridor to see what he could find in Mr Bunce's room.

Next to Karim's room was the bathroom that Tom had mentioned, with another bedroom next door. It was the same layout as Karim's but not in as tidy a state. A few clothes trailed along the floor, drawers were left open, and papers were scattered on the desk. Rufus had brought with him his most prized items from his prank collection—a small battery-operated toy snake that wriggled around on its own. He switched it on and placed it under the bed covers, hoping that the batteries would last long enough to scare the living daylights out of Mr Bunce. He watched with satisfaction as the outline of a snake slithered around under the covers.

Next, Rufus headed to the bathroom through a connecting door from Mr Bunce's room. He had brought with him red food colouring that he had intended to put into one of the toiletries bottles. However, he could only see a tube of toothpaste and wouldn't be able to squeeze the red dye in there. He looked around the bathroom at the toilet, the sink with a mirror above it and the bath with a shower head inside. Suddenly a marvellous idea occurred to him. He climbed into the bath and twisted the plastic fitting on the shower head until it came off in his hand. Taking out the red food colouring, he squeezed several drops into the back of the shower head and replaced the plastic cap. Now whoever had a shower next would have red water pouring down on them. Rufus chuckled to himself at the thought and rather hoped that Mr Bunce would take a shower before Karim.

To add the finishing touches, Rufus picked up a bar of soap and wrote a message in large letters on the bathroom mirror. He carefully wiped the message with toilet tissue so that the soap residue became invisible. Having played this trick once before on a school trip, Rufus knew that as soon as someone took a hot shower in the bathroom, the steam from the shower would make the words appear on the mirror again.

Feeling pleased with his efforts, he headed back downstairs to find the others.

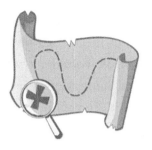

Chapter 22
Mr Bunce Flips

Rufus found Lara and Tom with Barney in the garden but would not be drawn into explaining his pranks.

Mrs Burt called them in to eat dinner. The kitchen smelled divine as Mrs Burt had prepared roast chicken, crispy roasted potatoes and all the trimmings. Barney was delighted to find that he had been given his own roast dinner in his dish by the back door. Mr Burt, Uncle Herb and Karim were at the table, but there was no sign of Mr Bunce.

"This all looks wonderful, Mrs Burt," said Karim, rubbing his hands together. "You sure are a brilliant cook."

"Thank you," said Mrs Burt, looking proud. "Did you find Mr Bunce to tell him that dinner is ready?"

"I saw him come in from the garden, he lost track of time. He should be here in a few minutes after he's freshened up."

Lara, Rufus and Tom resisted looking at each other, Rufus hoped that this meant that Mr Bunce was going to have a shower before coming downstairs for dinner. They eagerly chatted amongst themselves and asked Mr Burt questions about the greenhouse so that it would not look like they were waiting for something to happen.

Meanwhile upstairs, Mr Bunce was feeling remarkably pleased with himself. He knew that the children must be onto something and with Karim trailing their every move and reporting back to him, it would surely not be long before the treasure was in his hands. He wondered how to get rid of the children once he had stolen the next clue from them… perhaps he could convince their doddery old great-uncle to send them away if he offered him some pittance.

His enormous gut rumbled for his dinner, and he stepped into the bathroom to shower as quickly as possible. Once in the shower he closed his eyes and let the warm water rain down on him, imagining all the pleasant things he would be able to buy once he had stolen Captain Jack Kexley's treasure. A song popped into his head, and he began to sing it loudly.

Upon reaching the song's chorus, he opened his eyes.

"What is this?" he said to himself, noticing that his hands had turned red. "Blood?" His pulse quickened.

Mr Bunce screamed in terror as the red water rained down on him. He jumped out of the bath without switching the shower off and stared back at the water in horror and shock.

"I need to get out of here," he yelled aloud. Turning around he faced the mirror and saw large letters staring back at him:

GET OUT

THE CURSE WILL GET YOU

LEAVE NOW

Mr Bunce could not believe his eyes. He had heard about the curse surrounding the castle but was not a man to be deterred by what he believed to be fairy stories, especially when lots of money was at stake. Seeing the words in front of him was a different matter altogether. He grabbed a towel and hurried into his bedroom, blubbering. Pulling some of his clothes from the floor, he quickly got dressed with fumbling and shaking hands. Finally, pulling a polo shirt over his head, he noticed a movement out of the corner of his eye. Something was moving under his bedsheets. Feeling sick with apprehension, he wanted to look but was terrified to. He yanked the covers off the bed in one swift motion and jumped back in horror.

"Snake, *snake*," he shrieked, pelting out of the door and down the stairs as if the toy snake were able to jump up and chase him at sixty miles per hour.

Back downstairs in the kitchen, everyone heard a cry in the distance that was soon followed by Mr Bunce tearing into the room. His eyes were wild, and he clutched the kitchen worktop for support.

"Blood in the shower… the curse… snakes in my room…" he spluttered.

Everyone in the room looked at him, astonished.

"Are you feeling well, Bunce?" asked Uncle Herb.

"What's the matter with you, man?" asked Mr Burt, more bluntly.

"You do look a bit peaky," added Mrs Burt.

"I'm telling you…" gasped Mr Bunce. "*Blood* is coming out of the shower… and there's a snake in my bed." He covered his face with his hands.

A few moments passed while the other adults digested this news.

"Nonsense, Bunce," laughed Uncle Herb. "What are you talking about?"

"See for yourselves," Mr Bunce said, pointing to the door that led to the rooms.

Everyone quickly jumped up and followed Mr Bunce back upstairs to his bedroom and bathroom. Barney, who was equally curious and had finished his chicken dinner, followed suit.

The adults followed Mr Bunce into the bathroom and stared at the shower. The red food colouring drops had by now disappeared down the plug hole, and the water was looking perfectly normal.

"Th-th-th-there was *blood*," insisted Mr Bunce. "I'm telling you, there was blood cascading out of the shower," he said, wide-eyed with fear.

Mr Burt leaned in and turned the water off and on a few times—there was no evidence of any change of colour in the water.

While Mr Bunce continued protesting and the other adults wondered if he had gone mad, Rufus silently crept behind them and wiped the mirror with his sleeve, clearing the message he had written. He stepped back into the hall before anyone had turned around.

"It wasn't just the water, there was a message on the-" Mr Bunce stopped mid-sentence as he turned and saw a normal looking mirror, completely devoid of any threatening words.

"Well, the snake must still be there," he continued. "Follow me."

Everyone crowded into the bedroom where the covers were still thrown back, but there was no snake in sight.

"This is absurd, Bunce," scolded Uncle Herb.

"Our dinners are getting cold for this," complained Mr Burt.

While Mr Bunce insisted there had been a real live snake in his bed, Barney spotted a toy snake wriggling about in the corner of the room next to the door. He grabbed it gleefully and took it to Lara, who nimbly switched off the batteries and stuffed it into her pocket.

"Are you *sure* these things happened, Boss?" asked Karim.

Mr Bunce gave Karim an icy glare.

"Of *course* it all happened, Karim. Do you really think I'd make things up? Unless..." Mr Bunce turned towards Lara, Tom and Rufus. "*You,*" he spat. "You children had something to do with this."

Rufus put his hand on his chest and gasped.

"Mr Bunce, I must say I am shocked *and* appalled," he protested, sounding so innocent and hurt that it was a struggle for Lara and Tom to keep a straight face. "We were downstairs eating Mrs B's delicious cooking until you caused all this commotion."

Mrs Burt glowed at receiving another compliment on her cooking.

"It's true Boss, they were all downstairs until just now."

"Shut up," hissed Mr Bunce. "I will not stay here tonight… I am going to get a room at The Laughing Pig forthwith. Karim, I will be back first thing tomorrow morning. Continue with your… *tasks*."

Within the next few minutes, Mr Bunce had shoved his belongings in a bag and stormed out of the castle, slamming the heavy front door behind him. Everyone else returned to the kitchen to finish their dinners and a delicious peach cobbler that Mrs Burt had prepared for dessert.

The children assumed that Karim's 'tasks' consisted of following them about. Somehow, they thought to themselves, they had to get to the racecourse tomorrow without being spotted.

Chapter 23
Beginning the Race

The next morning their fears were confirmed as Karim seemed to be *everywhere*. When they woke up, he was passing the corridor outside their rooms, whistling. While they had breakfast, he was lurking outside the kitchen window pretending to be interested in the flowers planted in the window box. As Lara took Barney out for a run around the lawn, Karim appeared with an exercise mat and began a series of yoga poses. Even Barney was losing his patience and started to growl every time Karim popped up on the scene.

"I can't bear it anymore," said Lara to Tom and Rufus when she and Barney re-joined them back in the kitchen. "He's *everywhere.*"

Mrs Burt had prepared a picnic lunch for the children which Tom was packing into his backpack.

"Hello there," said Karim, popping his head through the door. "Heading out today?"

"Gaaaah," screamed Lara while throwing her hands up, unable to hide her exasperation anymore.

"Er, we're getting the bus into Cliffesville," answered Tom, ignoring Lara's outburst.

"That's nice. What are you going to–"

Before Karim could complete his question, he was interrupted by the booming voice of Mr Bunce calling his name from the front door.

The moment Karim disappeared they were seized with the same impulse.

"Leg it," cried Tom as he grabbed his backpack and charged out of the back door, followed by Rufus, Lara and Barney. Tom grabbed his bike and helmet from outside his cottage. They did not look back as they pelted out of the castle gates and barely stopped for breath until they reached the cycle hire shop. At each moment they expected to see Mr Bunce's black Peugeot rolling down towards the village to spy on them. Once Lara and Rufus had paid for their bikes and helmets, Tom showed them a map he had printed from his computer, and they started their journey to the racecourse.

Passing fields and woods, Lara and Rufus enjoyed the freedom of whirring through the countryside in the fresh breeze. Before long they arrived at Polwellan Racecourse—a large abandoned grey building, littered with broken glass and graffiti.

Rufus read a notice attached above the main entrance.

DANGEROUS – KEEP OUT

PUBLIC NOTICE OF DEMOLITION

COMING SOON – POLWELLAN PRIORY ESTATE

Next to the notice was a flyer with a picture of a housing development that the old racetrack was to become.

"Maybe we shouldn't go in there," said Tom. "We could get ourselves blown up with the building."

All three were feeling apprehensive.

"Wait a second," said Lara. "There's a date on the demolition notice… the second of August…"

"That's tomorrow," said Rufus, relieved. "We've got time, come on."

Tom and Lara glanced at each other, still feeling nervous.

"Come on guys," continued Rufus. "If this place were being demolished today there'd be security everywhere and bulldozers."

"There might still be security here," said Lara.

"We'll have to be really careful," said Tom. "My mum would kill me if she knew we were even standing outside this place."

"This is our last chance," pleaded Rufus. "If we don't get the clue today, this place will be gone tomorrow, and we'll never find the treasure. Herb will lose the castle if Bunce doesn't buy it from him for peanuts."

Nobody liked the thought of losing the treasure or the castle.

"Let's go in," agreed Lara, "but the moment it gets dangerous, we need to get out of there."

The front entrance was locked so they walked around the building to look for an opening. Where the building stopped a large wall circled the racetrack, too high for any of them to climb. They circled the site looking for a hole or opening, but found themselves back at the main entrance again.

"Up there," said Lara. "That window to the side above the doors doesn't have any glass… can one of us get through?"

"I don't think I could," said Tom. "It's tiny."

"I'll do it," volunteered Rufus, who was the shortest and skinniest of the three, despite consuming three times as much food.

Tom hoisted Rufus onto his shoulders, and he quickly scrambled up and squeezed into the window with ease.

"Find a way to let us in," called Lara.

Tom and Lara moved their three bikes behind a large bush, so that they were out of sight for anyone entering or leaving the building.

Meanwhile, Rufus found himself in what looked like it had once been an office. All of the furniture had gone, but a noticeboard still remained on the wall with messages on yellow paper stuck with drawing pins and an old-fashioned telephone hung on the wall. Rufus headed out of the doorway. In front of him were a metal staircase and another room looking out over the racecourse. He headed to where the viewing windows would have been and looked out, wondering whether his ancestor Captain Jack Kexley had once stood in the same spot to watch the races. As his imagination conjured images of the past, he was jolted back to the present by a voice calling his name.

"Hurry up, Rufus," called Lara from downstairs. "Let us in."

Rufus walked down the metal staircase to the large entrance. With considerable effort, he was finally able to slide the stiff bolts and push the doors open.

Lara, Tom and Barney hurried inside. Tom closed the door behind them and slid the bolts across.

"We've got to find the willow tree," said Lara.

"Shhh," hushed Tom. "Other people could be in here."

Trying to make as little noise as possible, they headed down a dark corridor that curved around the outside of the track.

Suddenly Tom stopped in his tracks and put a hand out to warn Rufus and Lara. Each of them could hear voices and the sound of footsteps getting closer. Barney let out a sharp bark. Lara quickly grabbed his collar and opened the door to her left, pulling him into the room followed by Rufus and Tom.

They were in what appeared to be another spectator's room leading to an outdoor viewing platform. The voices started to become audible.

"Did you hear that dog, Marvin?" asked one of the voices.

"No... as if there'd be a dog in here, you muppet," said Marvin.

"I'm telling you, I heard a dog barking."

"Jake... if I've told you once I've told you a thousand times, there is no such thing as a haunted racecourse."

"No," said Jake. "It wasn't one of them ghost sounds this time, it sounded real."

"First you hear ghost horses, now a real dog… you want to get your head examined."

"Can we just check it out? I *know* I didn't make it up."

"Fine, we'll check these rooms, and if there's nothing there, lunch is on you."

Lara, Tom, Rufus and Barney had gone onto the viewing platform and were hiding behind a pillar between the two rooms. Lara kept her hand on Barney's collar to warn him not to make another sound. They heard doors being opened and shut and footsteps moving. Suddenly the door to their room was slung open. Lara felt her heart thumping in her chest as the footsteps came nearer. She hoped with all her might that a foot or elbow wasn't poking out the side of the pillar.

"See—nothing here, you turnip," yelled Marvin.

"But I heard it," cried Jake, who was still searching in every direction.

"Enough already. Let's go to Tina's, and you can buy me a bacon sandwich. We'd better go now so we can get back here before the boss gets back."

The two men left the room, and slowly the sound of footsteps faded. The remaining three breathed sighs of relief.

"We really can't stay here long, they'll be back in a few minutes," said Lara. "We passed Tina's café, and it's only down the road from here."

"How do we know where to look?" asked Rufus, looking around the room. "This place is gigantic."

"Over there," Tom pointed to the far end of the race course. "There's a willow tree… and I think I can see a plaque or something on the ground."

Chapter 24
The Final Clue

Lara, Tom, Rufus and Barney climbed down the spectator stand onto the race track. The willow tree looked strangely out of place on the dry and dusty track. The children read the metal plaque on the ground beneath the tree:

Here lies the remains of Lord Anthony, 1853 – 1877.

Five-time Polwellan Cup Winner.

"That's it?" asked Rufus, crestfallen. "How can that be a clue?"

"There must be something else around here," said Lara, who got up to search around the back of the willow tree. Rufus and Barney joined her; Barney was not quite sure what everyone was looking for, but eagerly sniffed around to help.

Tom stared down at the plaque, noticing the four rusty metal screws. He tapped the metal, which sounded hollow underneath. Taking out his keyring which had a small screwdriver attached, he worked at removing the metal screws. Although it was not quite the right size, he managed to remove them from the plaque. He placed his fingers around the plaque, and it lifted easily from the ground, revealing a metal box below.

"Hey guys, check this out," Tom yelled to Rufus and Lara. They were quickly at his side as he pulled a wooden box out of the metal space—identical to the boxes containing the first two clues. They gasped and whooped for joy, thrilled at their discovery. As Tom opened the box, he pulled out a piece of parchment paper containing a map.

The map showed turrets on one side, which looked like it symbolised the castle. In the middle of the turrets was a picture of an Egyptian king and queen. A dotted line ran from the queen down to the cliffs and the water.

"They look like the statues of the Egyptian king and queen in the castle entrance," Lara pointed out. She could not remember a time when she had ever been this excited. For years she had been prone to treating situations with suspicion and mistrust—particularly ones that involved Rufus. Since her arrival at the castle, she was beginning to feel more confident as part of a group, all striving towards the same goal.

"There must be some sort of passage around there that goes down to the beach… maybe even under the sea," said Rufus.

"There's some words in the corner," said Lara, noticing very small and curled handwriting on the map.

From Nefertiti to the sea, follow the way,

To fame, fortune, my life's riches, yet stay,

Ahead of the tide, for danger is near,

A suit will lead you to all I held dear.

"Who's Nefertiti?" asked Rufus.

"She was an Egyptian queen and the wife of Akhenaten," explained Lara. "They worshipped Aten, which was the sun."

"We can't sit here and work it all out," cautioned Tom as he looked around to see if the security guards had returned. "I'll put these screws back in, so it looks the same."

Lara, Rufus, Tom and Barney quickly made their way back to the spectator stand and climbed back into the room. Before they exited into the corridor, they heard a voice that was disturbingly close.

"I'll show him I'm not making things up," murmured Jake to himself, as he flung each door open.

They did not have time to hide back in the stands and stared at each other in horror as the door of the room next door was thrown open, and footsteps pounded towards the spot where they stood.

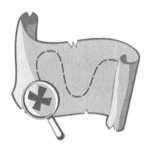

Chapter 25
Back to the Castle

There was no time to lose, something had to be done. A hand moved the handle of the door and Rufus was spurred into action.

"Hhhhhrrtrmmmppppphhhh," he cried, mimicking a horse with surprising accuracy. "Hhhhrrrrrmmmppph."

"Who's there?" called Jake, sounding nervous.

Tom joined in the whinnying and Lara mimicked horse footsteps clop-clopping on the ground. In a moment it sounded like several horses were charging towards the door. Barney threw his head back and howled, sounding like a wolf. The combined effect was extremely disturbing.

"Not this again," wailed poor Jake, his hands covering his ears. "Get away. Ghosts, ghosts after me. Marvin…. *Marvin!*"

Jake ran back down the corridor to find his colleague. They ran as fast as they could out of the main entrance and retrieved their bikes from the hiding spot in the bush, hurling themselves onto them.

"Good thinking with the horse noises," said Tom once they had peddled a safe distance away.

"He probably owes Marvin two lunches now," observed Lara.

"I'm getting really hungry," complained Rufus. "Let's stop somewhere and have our lunch."

They stopped at a wooded area. Tom unpacked the lunch that his mother had prepared—heaps of sandwiches with three different fillings. There was also homemade cheese and onion quiche, a big bag of salted crisps and slabs of carrot cake for dessert. Lara poured some water into a dish for Barney.

"I think we should go and find the treasure tonight," suggested Rufus, in between bites of quiche. "If we go in the daytime Karim will be following us again."

"It's too dangerous," advised Tom. "The high tide is tonight, and we might not be able to see it catch up with us in the dark."

"Didn't the map say something about a tide as well," remembered Lara, looking at the map again. "'Stay ahead of the tide, for danger is nigh'—Grandad said something about the tide as well when he dropped us off."

"It can be really bad," said Tom. "The current is strong too; a few people have got in trouble out swimming."

"Ok, so we'll go early in the morning then," persisted Rufus. "I've got a bad feeling about Bunce… I wonder what he's been up to at the castle today."

"Probably having a go at Karim for letting us leave," said Lara. "I would feel sorry for him if he wasn't so annoying, turning up everywhere."

"He's not as bad as Bunce," said Tom. "That guy is a crook."

When they returned to the castle that afternoon, they saw that Mr Bunce had been very busy indeed. A team of workmen were buzzing all over the castle and grounds, making inspections. Karim was standing apart from all the activities, looking very sorry for himself after having received yet another scathing telling-off from Mr Bunce.

"What's going on?" Tom asked his father as he entered the hall to join them.

"That Bunce chap has paid Herb to allow these goons to search all over the place for signs of hidden passages and the like," Mr Burt explained. "He doesn't think they'll find anything meaningful and he can't turn down any easy cash right now."

"Why all these people?" asked Lara.

"They've brought special equipment to try and detect any hollow spaces. All a load of codswallop if you ask me. Next thing you know we'll have the flamin' Ghostbusters coming round to search the place!"

"Where's Herb now?" questioned Rufus.

"He cleared off this morning shortly after Bunce arrived. Some of these workers are a bit ham-fisted, and it upsets him seeing people messing about with the place."

At that moment, one of the workers was standing on a chair to inspect a painting of a lady on the wall. As he attempted to look behind it, he accidentally unhooked the picture, and it tumbled straight onto Mr Bunce's head, knocking him down to the ground. His face had pierced straight through the portrait where the lady's head had been.

"*Owww*. Get this off me you lumbering idiots," he cried, looking ridiculous.

"Hey Bunce," yelled Rufus. "Your face is a picture."

Tom, Lara and Mr Burt could no longer stifle their laughter.

Mr Bunce snarled and growled in response as the workers started to yank the painting off his head. Even Karim began to laugh until Mr Bunce glared savagely at him.

"I see what you mean about ham-fisted," said Tom to his father.

"Was it a valuable painting?" Lara asked Tom.

"No, the only original ones are in the gallery," Tom answered. "That one is a print of one that was sold two years ago. And good job too."

They left Mr Bunce scolding the workers and headed upstairs to Lara's room.

"If we start looking for the treasure around breakfast time those workmen will see us," said Lara.

"Yeah, it's hard enough giving Karim the slip without a whole team of Bunce's buffoons as well," said Rufus.

"Let's meet at around four," proposed Tom. "The tide should start to go back out again then, and I guess those people will turn up at around eight."

"We're so close," said Lara, beaming with excitement. "I can just *feel* it."

Tom imagined how happy his mother and father would be if he were able to discover the treasure with his new friends. It could mean a huge weight lifted for his family if they could continue living at the castle without the stresses and strains of not being able to make enough money to get by. He wanted that for them more than anything else he could wish for.

"I'm so happy you guys came here to stay," he told the others. "Nothing like this has ever happened to me before… I really want us to do this."

"I'm happy too," said Lara. "I was so angry at first that mum changed our holiday plans, but it's been the biggest adventure me and Barney have ever had."

Barney barked in agreement.

Lara and Tom looked at Rufus, wondering if he would say something equally heartfelt.

"I'm happy it's dinnertime soon," he said, truthfully.

Lara groaned.

"All you think about is food and pranks," she said.

"And video games" Rufus added. "And treasure. Oh, and zombies. And–"

"Oh, come on," interrupted Lara, "let's go and eat."

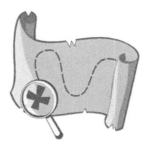

Chapter 26
The Treasure Hunt Begins

Rufus, Lara and Tom did not stay up late after dinner, although it was difficult to sleep when they were all so excited. Lara's alarm buzzed at three o'clock, and she sprung out of bed, eager to start the treasure hunt.

After a quick wash, she went downstairs to the kitchen to feed Barney, where she found Rufus busy raiding the fridge and cupboards.

"In case we get hungry later," he explained.

At four o'clock and while it was still pitch-black outside, they met Tom in the hallway next to the statue of Queen Nefertiti. He handed a torch each to Lara and Rufus.

They shined their torches all around the statue, but could not see anything.

"What if there's something higher up?" whispered Lara, not wanting to wake anyone else in the household.

"Hoist me up and I'll look," said Rufus.

Tom gave Rufus a leg up, and he shuffled his way up the statue. He gripped the front of the head and felt something shift.

"Lara, what's my hand on?" he asked with excitement. "I felt something move."

"It's a jewel on her headdress," said Lara. "Something happened down here too; move it again."

Rufus carefully moved the jewel as far as it would go. The entire statue began to slide backwards with a low grating sound. Rufus almost lost his balance and Lara put a hand on Barney's collar to stop him barking.

The statue had revealed a large opening in the floor. Stone stairs led down into the darkness. The three shone their torches into a long tunnel.

"It's veering off towards the direction of the sea," said Tom. He noticed a lever next to him and pulled it. The large statue ground back into place over their heads until the tunnel was completely hidden.

"Hopefully Bunce's lot won't spot that the jewel moves," he said.

"Well, at least we'll get a good head start on them if they do," said Lara.

They walked down the dark, narrow tunnel for around twenty minutes.

"Oh, hang on," cried Lara, holding her head in her hands. "Oh no!"

"What's up?" asked Rufus.

"When we went upstairs last night, we took the box and map with us… it's still there."

"Well we can't go back now," said Tom. "We'll still get there first even if they go snooping and find the map."

"Look," exclaimed Rufus. "The ground and walls are wet. They weren't further up. And the ceiling looks damp too."

The tunnel was becoming very slippery and Barney began to skid and slide in front of the children.

"I don't like this," said Tom. "This place must've been full of seawater recently… it must be the tide. Maybe we should head back?"

"Let's give it five minutes," said Lara. "If we don't reach the end by then we'll turn around."

As they walked for another few moments, light began to appear at the end of the tunnel, much to their relief. Barney raced ahead eagerly, glad to reach fresh air.

The tunnel opened into a tiny and very rocky cove, surrounded by steep cliffs on each side.

"We can't be out here long," said Tom, who was feeling anxious. "See this mark?" He pointed high above his head where the cliff became lighter in colour. "That's how high up the water comes in high tide. And it's coming in now."

"How long do you think it would take?" asked Lara.

"From where the sea is now… it would reach that tunnel in less than two hours."

"That's loads of time," cried Rufus, who could not bear the thought of returning to the castle empty-handed.

They began to explore the small cove. Directly opposite the tunnel, there was a rocky ledge around half a metre from the ground.

"Over there," yelled Rufus.

Barney jumped onto the ledge, Tom, Lara and Rufus climbed up after. Another cave passage stretched in front of them.

"This must be the way," said Lara.

They hurried down the passage which was still wet and covered in green slimy seaweed. Minutes later, the tunnel opened out into a square space, with no way forward.

"A dead end," observed Lara, her heart sinking.

"Maybe we picked the wrong cave?" said Rufus.

"I didn't see any others," said Tom. "Although... do you see that crack down the rock? Maybe there's a way to get through..."

In the rocky wall opposite where the children stood there was a straight line running down the centre.

"Maybe there's a clue somewhere..." said Lara. "Everywhere is covered in seaweed. Let's move some of it."

Tom, Lara and Rufus began to peel and scoop the slimy, smelly seaweed from the walls, dumping it into a pile in the middle of the room.

"I can see something," Rufus yelled. Tom and Lara helped him to clear the remaining seaweed and debris from his area to reveal small stone squares against a ledge. Each square had a letter carved deep into the stone. There were twenty-six in total to represent each letter of the alphabet.

"What do we do with these?" wondered Tom.

"There has to be something else here," said Lara. "Keep looking, there's still time."

They went back to pulling the seaweed from the walls. Rufus was eagerly dumping an armful into the centre when he slipped, falling face down into the large pile of green congealed weeds.

"Pah," he said, spitting seaweed out of his mouth. "This stinks."

Tom and Lara burst into laughter as Rufus wrestled with mounds of green slop.

"I am the sea monster," he shouted, waving his hands and shooting strands of seaweed directly at his cousin and Tom. Barney was delighted at this game and threw himself onto Rufus, covering them both in even more seaweed.

"Let's get them, sea dog," Rufus hollered, still flinging green debris onto Tom and Lara. "Pow, pow. Take *that*."

"Come on you two, stop mucking about," said Lara. "You're not helping."

Soon they got back to work, and Lara made a breakthrough.

"There's something here," she exclaimed. She had uncovered a shelf on the wall opposite the letters that had five spaces the same size as the small tiles.

"We need a five-letter word!" she said.

"Farts?" suggested Rufus.

"Still not helping," Lara rolled her eyes. Each of them tried hard to think of a word that could fit into the spaces.

"Burps?" suggested Rufus, after a few minutes of silence. Tom groaned.

"Stop being a joker," he said.

"Joker... that's it..." said Lara, an idea forming in her head.

"Joker?" said Tom. "It's five letters but why would the password be joker?"

"Joker is a card..." said Lara. "This whole time the clues have been linked to playing cards... the Jack of Hearts was in the globe, it was on the wall in The Laughing Pig... it was in the diary... and the map said a *suit* would lead us... he meant a suit of cards. The secret word is *heart*."

"That's brilliant," cried Rufus. "You've got it, Lara."

"Let's get the letters," said Tom.

They raced to pick up the letters and placed them in order on the shelf.

"What now, Lara?" Rufus asked as they waited expectantly.

"You can't expect me to work out everything," Lara replied.

Rufus looked around but could not see any sort of lever. He felt around the shelf attempting to slide it, but it would not budge. Then he leant his weight against the shelf, and to his delight, it shot backwards deeper into the wall, and a noise began to rumble.

"The wall is opening, we did it," he said, jumping with excitement.

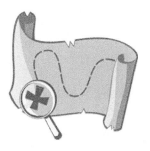

Chapter 27
Captain Jack Kexley's Treasure

They watched in amazement as the walls slowly opened to reveal a small gap. Lara walked in first and shone her torch around the hidden room.

"Can you see anything?" asked Rufus, fighting the impulse to push his cousin out of the way.

"Yes," said Lara, smiling. "Wonderful things." Now she knew how Howard Carter must have felt when he first entered Tutankhamen's tomb.

All three were now shining their torches inside the secret room. A dazzling sight met their eyes. Masses of shining Egyptian statues, masks, weapons, furniture and jewellery, from one end of the room to the other. They felt as if they had stepped back into ancient times; almost visualising the craftsmen labouring hard to construct these treasures thousands of years ago.

"Gold," whispered Rufus. "Everything… is gold." He had spent a lot of time daydreaming about the treasure since their search began, but even in his wildest imaginings he could not have pictured the sight in front of his eyes.

"It doesn't feel real," said Tom. "I feel like we're trespassing."

"You *are*," boomed a loud, odious voice from behind them.

The three turned around in shock. Standing in front of the entrance was Mr Bunce, holding a revolver, along with five of the workmen who had been causing havoc in the castle hallway the day before.

Barney barked and moved forward to lunge at Mr Bunce; Lara grabbed hold of his collar just in time.

"Keep hold of that mutt before I shoot him," said Mr Bunce. "Right, over there against the wall, all of you. Wallace, point your gun at them while we take a look inside here. If one of them moves, shoot them."

Lara, Tom and Rufus left the room full of treasure and lined up against the wall in the seaweed room. They all felt sick with disappointment.

Meanwhile, Mr Bunce and four of the workers entered the treasure room. Lots of yelps and screams of excitement echoed out into the tunnel, mainly from Mr Bunce.

"Whooo. Glorious. Aha. *Magnificent.* Yipee. Splendid… superb… I'm *rich.*"

Rufus had been caught out in his pranks and schemes many times by teachers, grandparents and other figures of authority—but he had never felt quite as wretched as he did at that moment, forced to listen to Mr Bunce whooping and hollering for joy.

Mr Bunce re-emerged, looking as happy as a fat pig sloshing about in a river of mud.

"We'll leave it all here for now until we can get a boat to transport everything," he said. "Then we can get this out onto the black market. I'm going to–"

Mr Bunce stopped mid-sentence as a rumbling sound started up behind him. The door of the treasure room was closing and the tablets spelling the letter 'heart' sprung out of the wall and fell straight onto the floor. Moments later, water began seeping into the tunnel where they stood.

"The tide, it's come in already. Let's get out of here," wailed Mr Bunce.

Mr Bunce and his men ran out of the tunnel, followed behind by Tom, Rufus, Lara, and Barney. When they reached the cove, most of the beach and rocks except for a tiny strip next to the cliff had been covered by the sea. The tunnel leading from the castle was completely submerged in water. They waded in water higher than their waists to follow the men to the dry piece of land. Barney paddled in the water next to Lara.

Once safely on dry land, one of Mr Bunce's men removed some climbing equipment from his rucksack. Within minutes, he had made his way to the top of the cliff and attached a rope ladder that he threw down for the others to climb.

"What do we do with the kids?" Wallace asked Bunce.

"Leave them here," spat Mr Bunce. "Nasty little brats."

"What?" cried Tom. "You can't. The tide is coming in, and nobody could swim against that current."

"So much the better," said Mr Bunce, smiling venomously. "You'll be off the scene, and it will look like a swimming accident. I'm going up, Wallace—if any of these kids try to follow us up the ladder, shoot them."

Mr Bunce and the remaining workers climbed to the top of the cliff, pulling the rope ladder up behind them. They disappeared out of sight.

Barney barked as the waves climbed higher and higher.

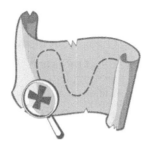

Chapter 28
In Trouble

"Isn't there any other way we can get out?" said Lara, frantically searching the cliffs for any possible way to climb out of danger.

"Not that I can see," said Tom looking around in a panic.

"Can we swim for it?" Lara asked.

"We could try... but look over there at how fast that current is moving."

Tom pointed past the underwater tunnel where a current of water was ripping through the sea at tremendous speed, smashing against the rocks.

"We'll just have to try and wait it out as long as possible," said Lara, feeling grim. "Then somehow stay afloat until the tide goes back out again."

Tom's heart sank as he knew that it took several hours for the tides to change, but he did not see the value in telling the others at that moment.

Minutes passed in silence and despair. By then, they were standing in water up to their ankles as the waves hit their knees. Barney jumped in surprise every time a large wave struck.

Rufus reached into his backpack.

"Anyone want a biscuit?" he asked.

"*How* can you think of eating at a time like this?" Lara shrieked.

"Well, if we're all going to die, I don't want to die hungry," he replied.

More time passed, and the waves leapt higher and higher.

"Tom, help me hold Barney," said Lara. "He's almost underwater."

They picked up the nervous and frightened dog, holding him in their arms above the water.

"This is so awful," cried Lara. "Rufus... you're not *still* eating?"

"It helps take my mind off it," yelled Rufus, shoving another biscuit into his mouth.

A noise started to hum in the distance. Soon it got louder until an extremely welcome sight appeared around the bay.

"A boat!" shouted Tom. "Quick, get their attention," he said, throwing an arm in the air.

The children shouted as loudly as they possibly could, waving their arms wildly. A man in the boat spotted them and to their immense relief, steered the small motorboat towards them.

As it came closer, they were able to see the face of their rescuer.

"Karim?" they yelled in unison and utter shock.

"I can't get right up to the cliff," called out Karim. "Can you manage to swim out a little bit?"

The children swam a few metres out to the motorboat, and the young man helped them in one-by-one, finally heaving Barney into the boat with effort. Moments later, he had navigated the boat through the rocks and was speeding along the Cornish coastline.

"Karim…" said Rufus. "We're all… really… glad you're here… I mean, *really*… but, what *are* you doing here?"

Karim sighed.

"Bunce is a crook," he said. "I came to the British Museum for research to finish my thesis; I never wanted any of this. Bunce said if I didn't come to Cornwall and help him, he would write to my university supervisor in Cairo and give me a bad report to make me fail my assignment. It was bad enough having to snoop around following you guys all the time, but when the workmen discovered the tunnel under Queen Nefertiti's statue this morning, I heard Bunce telling them that if they came across you in the tunnel, they would 'get rid' of you. I knew I had to do something. I made myself scarce so I wouldn't have to go with them, then I looked in your rooms and found the box with the map. I saw that the tunnel led underground; I also saw the warning about tides. I went down to the beach and spoke to that old man, Sam. He said that there are loads of tunnels inside the cliffs—even some by the castle beach—but that they're dangerous and get flooded by the tides."

"So that's where Barney kept running off to on the beach," interrupted Lara. "He kept disappearing on the castle's beach. Even Sam came out of nowhere one day."

"Anyway," continued Karim. "I knew it would be a bad idea to follow you all down the tunnel—I'd either run straight into Bunce or be underwater. So, I ran down to the harbour as quickly as I could and hired this boat. I saw Bunce and the workmen walking at the top of the cliffs back towards the castle, and I knew he'd left you kids somewhere since you weren't with him. I'm so happy I found you."

"Not as happy as we are," said Rufus.

Lara looked at Karim and felt slightly guilty for all of the times she had felt severely irritated by him following them around. Suddenly a thought occurred to her.

"Wait! Stop the boat," she shouted.

Karim stopped so abruptly that Rufus almost flew out of the boat back into the water.

"What's up with you?" he asked Lara.

"If we go back to the castle Bunce and his gang might see us from the cliff," she explained. "We've got to let them think we drowned. If they think we're alive, they'll get away, and the police won't catch them."

"Have they actually committed a crime yet?" asked Tom. "I know Bunce stole the painting… but we don't have any proof, and it's being sent back."

"I can talk to the police about that," said Karim. "He also impersonated a police officer on the telephone to your uncle."

"They'll be going back for the treasure when the tide goes back out," said Rufus. "If the police met them there, they could catch them trying to steal the treasure to sell to the black market."

"I was wondering," said Lara. "How do you think the walls of the treasure cave closed on their own? It was really spooky."

"I was thinking about that too," said Tom. "There must be some sort of tool that triggers the doors closing once the water has reached a certain level. That stops all the treasure being washed away or ruined by sea water."

"Ingenious man, your ancestor," observed Karim.

Karim turned the boat around and they headed back towards the harbour in the opposite direction to the castle. Once there, Karim returned the boat to its owner, and they walked into the local police station.

"Tom," bellowed the officer at the desk, who knew the Burts well. "I've had your mother ringing up today saying the whole lot of you have been missing all day. I told her you'd likely all gone off somewhere together. I'll give Mrs Burt a ring now."

"I think you'd better wait for a bit," said Tom, worried his mother would give the game away to Mr Bunce. "We've got a lot to tell you."

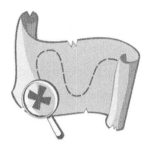

Chapter 29
The Final Mission

The policeman took Lara, Rufus, Tom, Karim and Barney into his office and listened to their story from start to finish. He gasped in amazement at the adventure the children had had.

"Well," said the policeman after he had finished pages and pages of notes. "I can't say we've ever had anything like this before, Tom... I need to get on the blower to my superior and see if we can get a squad down to the cove to catch those criminals."

"Can we come?" asked Rufus, who wanted nothing more than to see the look on Mr Bunce's face once he was caught.

"Well... we'll either have to take you with us or leave you here," said the policeman. "Unfortunately, as this is a live police operation the fewer people that see you out and about the better."

The policeman left and returned a few moments later.

"I've spoken to the boss," he said. "There's another four hours to go until the tide goes back out; we'll send a squad round to be there ahead of when Bunce and his lot come back. One of you can come with us to show us where the treasure cave is and how to get in—the rest will stay here until we've got the crooks locked up."

"What about me?" asked Karim. "Bunce doesn't know I rescued the kids… what if I went back to the castle and kept an eye on things?"

"Good idea," said the policeman. "If you can, try to get a message through to us when you see them leaving; I'll give you a number. But don't give the game away to anyone. Now, which of you kids is coming with us?"

All three paused for a moment, each desperately wanted to go with the police.

"You can let me know in a minute," said the policeman, not receiving an answer from anyone. "I need to make another phone call." He left the room along with Karim, who was going to make his way back to the castle.

"Lara, you should go," said Rufus, to her amazement. "I know I've been a pain at your house, with all the pranks… I just get bored sometimes… You deserve to go. You figured out the puzzle in the cave. You've always been the smart one."

"Thanks Rufus," said Lara, still shocked. "But I think I should stay here with Barney. He'll wonder what's going on if I disappear for a few hours and leave him here. What about you, Tom?"

"You deserve to go Tom," Rufus interrupted. "This place is your home, and you work so hard to help your parents." It was the first time in Rufus' life that he had consciously put others' needs before his own. Surprisingly, it didn't make him feel like he was missing out.

"Thank you, both of you," Tom said while looking down, he always found it hard to be the centre of attention. "I couldn't ask for better friends than you two."

Within the next few hours, Tom left the harbour with fifteen police officers and guided them to the rocky cove. Five police officers stayed in the boat and drove it some distance away. They wanted to make sure that Mr Bunce had no opportunity to get away. Tom showed the remaining policemen the two tunnels in the cove. The water had receded to just below the ledge of the treasure cave; they entered, and Tom opened the cave wall with the letters.

"I think five of us will wait in here," said the police officer in charge. "Bob, you take four men down to that other tunnel leading back to the castle. Once the tide has fully gone out, you can wait in there. We'll surprise Bunce's gang from the front when they open the wall, and you can surround them from the back."

Bob and four other policemen closed the wall by removing the letters and then concealed themselves ahead of Bunce's arrival.

Meanwhile, Karim had returned to the castle. Mr and Mrs Burt and even Uncle Herb were very worried about the children, but Karim did not dare to reveal anything. Mr Bunce was in such high spirits that he forgot Karim had not been around all day. Karim managed to telephone the police to tip them off, before boarding a large boat that had arrived at the castle beach to pick up Mr Bunce and the workmen.

Once the boat had arrived near the cove, Mr Bunce, Karim and four of the workmen got into a rowing boat to reach the shore. Mr Bunce led the way, excitedly opening the cave wall with the password and rushing into the treasure room. In a moment he was grabbed by a strong pair of arms and handcuffed. The four workmen tried to return through the tunnel where they were met by the other group of police officers who wrestled them to the ground. Tom, who had also been hiding in the cave, joined Karim to stand at the side.

They watched with amusement as Mr Bunce lost his temper.

"This is outrageous," he cried. "This was all Karim's idea, he orchestrated everything." Mr Bunce had not noticed that Karim was not being arrested by the policeman.

"We know all about your activities, Mr Bunce," said one of the police officers. "Save it for when you have a lawyer—you'll need one."

The police waiting in the boat arrested the two men from Bunce's gang who were waiting in the large boat, and the criminals were all taken to the police station. As the castle tunnel was now clear, one policeman walked with Tom and Karim back through the damp secret passage towards the castle. They arrived at the wooden bridge outside the castle entrance at the same time as a police car was pulling into the drive with Rufus and Lara.

Tom's parents and Uncle Herb rushed out of the castle to greet them, looking extremely relieved.

"What on earth has been going on?" asked Mrs Burt. "We've been at our wits' end! Lara, your mother is on a flight back from Egypt."

"We found the treasure Herb," yelled Rufus.

Uncle Herb stared in amazement.

"You what?" he cried. "It's not possible. It can't be possible..."

"The kids can tell you all about it," said the policeman, smiling. "I'll be back tomorrow as we'll need to get more information from you all. I'll also need to find someone who knows about all this Egyptian stuff to tell us what exactly is in that cave."

"My mum can do that," said Lara. "She's an Egyptologist and archaeologist. Hey Karim, maybe you can help too?"

"I would be honoured," said Karim with pride.

As the policemen were getting into the car, Tom walked over to have a quiet word.

"Karim won't get into trouble for this, will he?" he asked one of the officers. "He saved our lives today."

"No, not at all," the policeman replied. "Bunce is the man we want; the London Metropolitan Police have been looking into him for stolen museum objects. Karim has given us helpful information on Bunce; he won't be charged with anything."

Feeling relieved, Tom returned to the others.

"I'll cook you all a great big dinner," said Tom's mother with gusto. "Rufus, I bet you're hungry as a horse, as per usual."

"Urgh, please no," begged Rufus. "I'm *so* full," he said, rubbing his stomach.

"Well that's a first," said Tom. Everyone was stunned, apart from Lara.

"At the police station, they gave us takeaway menus and said we could have whatever we wanted" she explained. "So Rufus picked food from *three* different restaurants and ate it all. It was disgusting." She grimaced at the thought.

"No... more... food..." pleaded Rufus, clutching his stomach and walking over the bridge. "I need a lie-down!"

The others laughed and followed him into the castle.

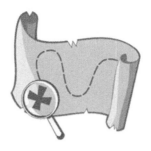

Chapter 30
The End of the Adventure

Lara, Rufus and Tom enjoyed telling Tom's parents and Uncle Herb about their adventure, although Tom wisely left out the part about the racecourse being scheduled for demolition. At the end of their tale, Uncle Herb asked them a question that he had been wondering all evening.

"Why didn't you tell me any of this was going on after we found the diary?" he asked, feeling a little offended.

"We wanted to, Uncle Herb," said Lara. "But we knew how much pressure you were under, and Bunce was paying you money. We didn't think you'd believe us."

Uncle Herb thought back to his early reluctance to having Lara and Rufus at the house and how much he had begrudged Rufus' destructive energy, in particular. He probably would not have trusted them, he thought to himself secretly, but everything would be different now.

"You've brought life back to this castle again," he said. "Both of you… and Barney too… you'll always be welcome here."

"What about the treasure?" asked Rufus. "Does it belong to you, Uncle Herb?"

"I wish," he answered, laughing. "That cove where you found the treasure is on public land. The treasures will be offered to a museum for exhibition."

"I guess it never really did belong to our family," Lara considered out loud. "Captain Jack Kexley took the treasure from Egypt; it was never his. A museum where everyone can enjoy it and learn from it is where it belongs now."

"Maybe that's the end of the castle's curse," said Rufus. "Returning the treasure where it belongs."

"Maybe my brother, your grandad, will be brave enough to step over the bridge next time he visits here," said Uncle Herb, laughing. He felt much lighter that evening than he had done for a long time, he thought. Maybe something truly had been lifted from the family.

"So… if the treasure is going to a museum… we're still broke?" asked Tom, who was feeling rather disappointed at this revelation.

"For now," said Uncle Herb. "But I have some ideas. I've still got quite a bit of money left over from that criminal Bunce, which we can use to repair the castle. Then perhaps we can open the place up next summer— take people in to look around on tours, maybe even take them on a mock treasure hunt."

"Herb," said Mr Burt, amazed at the personality transplant that he was witnessing. "I've suggested opening up the castle so many times, and you've *always* been dead set against it. You said it would spoil the place and you were opposed to the idea as a matter of principle."

"Sometimes one realises that some principles are less important than survival," Uncle Herb replied.

"I can open up a little café in the grounds," said Mrs Burt, who was eager for Uncle Herb not to be given long enough to change his mind.

"I can help too," said Tom. *Perhaps things aren't looking so hopeless after all*, he thought to himself.

"No, Tom," said Mrs Burt. "You've done so much for us already here, every day before and after school and during the holidays. Your dad and I, well we couldn't have asked for a better son. Not in a million years. It's time for you to enjoy some time with your friends, like all the other kids your age do."

"Maybe you could go and stay with Mrs Jacobs, Rufus, and Lara one summer. Or they could come and visit us here," suggested Mr Burt, smiling at his son.

"That would be great," said Tom. Before Lara and Rufus' arrival, he had spent all of his time outside classes helping with chores around the castle, mostly on his own. He didn't have time to make friends. "I'll still help though, as much as I can."

Later that evening, Mrs Jacobs called from London once her plane had arrived. Mrs Burt was pleased to tell her that the children were safe and well and put the phone to Lara who summarised everything that had happened.

Mrs Jacobs slept soundly in the airport hotel that night. She had gone through an extremely busy few days in Egypt working at the archaeological site, followed by a worrying journey back to England. Early in the morning, she phoned her supervisor in Egypt to explain that multitudes of lost ancient Egyptian artefacts had been discovered in Cornwall.

"Stay down there, Sarah," instructed her boss, with excitement. "Catalogue everything and report back. We'll get in touch with the Egyptian Ministry of State of Antiquities."

Later that morning after a long drive Mrs Jacobs arrived at Kexley Castle and was greeted warmly by everyone. She was told the finer details of the children's adventure and spent the next few days working with Karim—who she respected and got along well with—documenting and cataloguing each artefact in the cave in detail to report to the authorities. Lara, Rufus, and Tom enjoyed returning to the treasure cave and learning about each object and its history and origins.

Karim was the happiest he had been for a long time. He relished the opportunity to work on such an important discovery. After his studies were complete, Mrs Jacobs felt confident that he would be able to secure a teaching post in the London university where she worked.

A few government officials came to speak to Mrs Jacobs at the castle. The majority of the treasure would be transported to the Egyptian Museum in Cairo, whilst other items would be displayed in the British Museum in London.

News of the discovery was reported in newspapers and on TV stations all over the world, with reporters coming to the outside of the treasure cave to interview the castle's occupants.

A week after Mrs Jacobs arrived at the castle, everyone was having breakfast in the kitchen when a car pulled up outside the drive.

"More reporters?" asked Mrs Burt.

"I don't think so," said Uncle Herb. "Nobody has telephoned."

Everyone watched as a man opened the door for a woman in her early thirties. She tottered across the drive in a tight dress and high heels.

"Mum?" said Rufus. It had been over two years since he had seen Rachel, but she looked the same except for her long blonde peroxide hair being straight instead of curly. He stared in amazement.

"Come on," said Mrs Jacobs. "Let's go out and see your mum, Rufus."

Lara, her mother, Rufus and Tom went out to greet Rachel. She strode over to Rufus and enveloped him in an awkward-looking hug.

"Darling," she cried. "My *dear* boy."

"What are you doing here, Mum?" Rufus asked, stiffening his stance. He knew his mother wasn't here because she missed him.

"This is my friend, Ted Loxley" she answered. "He's a TV director. We've been so *excited* following your story, my boy. And I've got the *best* news ever! We're taking you to Los Angeles. Isn't that fantastic?"

Rufus stared at his mother in shock.

"I'm starting secondary school in September," he remonstrated. "I can't go with you."

Lara was flabbergasted.

"He *wants* to go to school?" she asked herself out loud. Her mother nudged her to keep quiet.

"Oh, never mind that!" said Rachel. I can get you a tutor on set. Ted here saw you on the news and thinks you'd be an absolute scream on kids' TV. Imagine being a big TV star. Isn't that just fabulous."

Rufus continued to stare wide-eyed in shock. Although she was his mother, he barely knew the woman. The thought of being pushed around a TV set all day by her and "Ted" was intolerable.

"I'm sorry Mum." he said, "but I'm not going."

"But you have to, darling, it's been arranged. I spoke to Grandma and Grandad, they want to take more holidays this year, so they can't be around to look after you all the time."

Lara felt awful for her cousin.

"This isn't right," she yelled. Everyone turned to her.

"Lara," said her mother gently, "Rufus' mum will decide what's for the best."

"But it's not for the best. He doesn't want to go. Can't he come and live with us?"

Now it was Rufus' turn to be stunned.

"Of course he can," said Mrs Jacobs. "But the two of you never got along with each other?"

"We do get along now," said Lara. "We've been through this whole adventure together."

Mrs Jacobs glanced at her sister, not knowing what to say. She did not want to undermine her sister's parenting responsibilities, but she also knew full well that Rachel had taken little interest in her son until now.

"Is that what you want?" Rufus' mum looked a little hurt. "To stay with your cousin and Auntie Sarah?"

"Yes," pleaded Rufus without a moment's hesitation. "Please, Mum."

Lara was beginning to feel sorry for her aunt. However, the feeling soon vanished when Rachel spoke.

"Well if that's what you want, so be it; we'll get some other kid for the show."

Ted opened the car door, and Rachel got in.

"Aren't you going to stay for a while?" asked her sister. "At least come inside?"

"We're *very* busy Sarah" she responded, whilst winding up the car window. "Cheerio, my boy. I'll be in touch."

The car rolled back out of the drive as unexpectedly as it had arrived.

Later that day the children were in the living room watching television.

Lara reflected on all the events of the past few days and how everything had turned out just right. Uncle Herb and the Burts had new income opportunities, and she, Rufus, Tom and Barney could all be together during the school holidays. Rufus would come to live with Lara, Barney and Mrs Jacobs full-time. He had been elated all day, sparking the return of speaking to everyone in a variety of accents, much to the annoyance of Mr Burt.

"Every time I hear that kid's voices, I keep thinking there's intruders in the place," he had complained frequently that day.

Lara's thoughts were interrupted when a picture of the children appeared on the TV screen.

"Now we join our reporter Maggie Mills," read the newsreader, "who earlier today was with the adventurers of the hour, Lara Jacobs, Rufus Kexley and Tom Burt, along with Barney the Border collie, who together have made the most significant discovery of Egyptian treasure in recent years..."

"Hey," exclaimed Rufus. "She called us 'The Adventurers'!"

"I like that," said Tom, smiling.

"I guess that's what we are?" said Lara. "This was a pretty big adventure. Do you reckon we'll have any more?"

Rufus beamed. "Anything is possible."

About the Author

Jemma Hatt grew up near Sevenoaks in Kent where she developed a passion for reading and writing short stories, which ultimately led to a degree in English Literature from the University of Exeter.

The Adventurers Series was inspired by many family holidays to Devon and Cornwall, as well as the adventure stories she loved reading as a child. After having lived and worked in London, New York and Delaware, Jemma is living in Kent and working on the next Adventurers stories as well as other writing projects.

Stay up-to-date with Jemma's writing and access free giveaways and offers by signing up to her newsletter at www.jemmahatt.com (if you are under 13 please ask an adult to sign up for you).

THE ADVENTURERS AND THE TEMPLE OF TREASURE

By Jemma Hatt

A father's legacy, a chase across Egypt and a mystery
buried for thousands of years...

... Lara, Rufus, Tom and Barney are back, in their
second exciting adventure together. With the help of
friends old and new, can they navigate their way
through the ancient wonders of Egypt to unearth one
of the greatest treasure troves in history?

THE ADVENTURERS AND THE CITY OF SECRETS

By Jemma Hatt

Two master criminals are on the run with ancient treasure, using London's web of hidden trails and passages to conceal their loot. The Adventurers must track them down using their wits, Uncle Logan... and a stolen red bus.

Join Lara, Rufus, Tom, Daisy and Barney as they race to uncover the City of Secrets!